STORM-BLAST

Curtis Parkinson

Tundra Books

Published in Canada by Tundra Books,
481 University Avenue, Toronto, Ontario M5G 2E9

Published in the United States by Tundra Books of Northern New York,
P.O. Box 1030, Plattsburgh, New York 12901

Library of Congress Control Number: 2002111525

National Library of Canada Cataloguing in Publication

Parkinson, Curtis
    Storm-blast/ Curtis Parkinson.

ISBN 0-88776-630-7

    I. Title.

PS8581.A76234S86 2003   JC813'.54   C2002-904143-0
PZ7

We acknowledge the support of the Canada Council for the Arts and the
Ontario Arts Council for our publishing program.

We acknowledge the financial support of the Government of Canada
through the Book Publishing Industry Development Program for our
publishing activities.

The poetry excerpts preceding the prologue and chapter openers
throughout the novel are taken from *The Rime of the Ancient Mariner*
(1798) by Samuel Taylor Coleridge (1772 – 1834).

Design: Terri Nimmo

Printed and bound in Canada

1 2 3 4 5 6   08 07 06 05 04 03

And now the Storm-blast came and he
Was tyrannous and strong

– from *The Rime of the Ancient Mariner*
by Samuel Taylor Coleridge

To Nancy

ACKNOWLEDGMENTS

My sincere thanks to the following:

Peter Carver and the George Brown writing group – where this all began as a short story – for their encouragement.

Anne Carter, Diana Aspin, and Helena for patiently reading, rereading, and making thoughtful suggestions as the short story grew into a novel.

Kevin Major and the Sage Hill workshop group, Joan Weir, Arthur Slade, Cathy Beveridge, Diane Salmon, and Sheena Kops for help and encouragement at a critical stage.

Finally, and most important, Kathy Lowinger for her insightful editorial advice, which gave the story new meaning, and Sue Tate for her careful and perceptive editing of the final manuscript.

Prologue

Alone, Alone, all, all alone,
Alone on a wide wide sea!

A river called the Don winds its way warily past the expressways, condos, and factories of eastern Toronto seeking the lake. At Bloor Street it flows under a bridge carrying thundering traffic. There, where the bicycle path took them, two boys stand among the willows at the water's edge. They would like to swim this endless, muggy July day, but the river is muddy and the signs warn of pollution.

Regan, the skinny one, tosses a piece of driftwood into the stream and watches it bob and twist until it's out of sight around a bend. "Hey, Matt, maybe it'll go all the way to the ocean," he ventures.

"Huh, not likely," Matt, the stocky one, snorts. Matt isn't given to long speeches. He selects a flat stone and skips it, wondering where his cousin Regan gets these crazy ideas.

In fact, Regan may be right – the driftwood just might make it to the ocean. For the Don will carry it into Lake Ontario, and from there it could be swept a thousand miles down the broad St. Lawrence – if it doesn't get hung up anywhere – and out into the Atlantic Ocean.

It might then, by a strange coincidence, be carried all the way to the Caribbean Sea. For one branch of the Atlantic current makes a vast clockwise sweep from Newfoundland east to the coast of France, then south to brush against Africa, then back west again until it reaches the Caribbean.

And suppose that piece of driftwood escapes being thrown up on one of the many Caribbean beaches. Then the current and the trade winds will keep taking it westward. On and on, across the empty expanse of the Caribbean Sea. A fate a piece of driftwood would have a good chance of surviving.

A much better chance than a boy. For a piece of driftwood doesn't need food and fresh water, and isn't likely to attract sharks.

1

A wicked whisper came, and made
My heart as dry as dust.

Thirty-seven. Regan touches the wall, pushes off, and begins the next lap. He has to keep repeating the number in his head, otherwise he starts thinking of something else and forgets by the time he reaches the other end. Forty lengths is his goal today. This is what he does best, the one thing he's good at – the *only* thing, he sometimes thinks. Stroking up and down the pool, getting a steady rhythm going, on and on, pretending he's training for the Olympic 1500-meter race. Not quite the same as the Olympics though because he has to keep swerving to avoid the other swimmers and the divers. On a hot July day, the big community pool is a popular place.

Reaching the other end, he catches a glimpse of Nick from his class talking to some of the guys. Nick's staring his way – not a good sign. He pushes off again. *Thirty-eight.*

At forty he stops, panting, resting his elbows on the edge. *Made it.* Nick's still there, beside the diving tower, still staring at him. Smirking's more like it. Among the group with him, Regan sees, is his cousin, Matt O'Brien.

· Matt strolls over. "Hey, Regan. What do you say we dive off the tower?" Matt puts one foot on the tower steps, ready to climb.

Regan shakes his head. "Naw, think I've had enough for today, Matt." He sounds offhand, but his insides churn when he thinks of diving from the tower, or even climbing that high.

Matt comes over, squats down beside him. He speaks quietly. "Listen, Regan, Nick says you're the only one of the guys who's never done it. Claims you don't have the guts. I said you do, and you could prove it."

"Geez, Matt, what did you do that for?"

"It's easy. Just climb up there and dive. Nothing to it."

Easy for you, Regan thinks. Anything like that is easy for Matt. Regan should know. He and Matt have been spending time together since they were little. Not because they particularly want to. Every summer, when it comes time for the annual family holiday, their two families rent a cottage, or go camping, or take a trip together. Always together. No one ever asks Regan or Matt how *they* feel about it.

"C'mon." Matt straightens, grabbing the rail leading

up. "You gotta show them *sometime*. Might as well do it now. Let's go."

Reluctantly, Regan hauls himself out of the pool, conscious that Nick and the others are watching his every move. Trying to appear casual, he almost takes a pratfall on the wet tiles, just managing to save himself by grabbing the rail. His arms and legs feel stiff and awkward, like a puppet's. He starts to climb. What choice does he have?

Anthony, he sees, is one of the group watching – his black skin standing out in sharp contrast to everyone else's. Anthony gives him an encouraging thumbs-up. One on his side anyway. The thought crosses Regan's mind that Anthony, too, knows what it's like to be odd man out.

He climbs slowly, step-by-step, hoping he can do it this time. He tried once before, one cool day when there was no one else around. He barely made it to the top before he had to turn back. Vertigo, it's called – he knows because a detective had it in a mystery story he read. Not that it does him much good to know what it's called. He wishes now he hadn't taken such care to hide it from everyone. Only his sister, Carol, suspects.

Ahead of him, Matt keeps going, past the intermediate level. Regan has his eyes fixed on the endless steps. He's sweating now, his skin clammy.

He reaches the top, steps shakily up onto the platform. *Don't look down.*

Matt stands calmly, toes curled around the edge, waiting for him. "Right after me. Okay?"

Regan holds the rail in a death grip. He watches as Matt sets himself, then launches into space, arms out in a swan dive. For a second Matt's body stays suspended in midair like a kite, then gravity takes over and he hurtles downward, drawing in his arms at the last second and entering the water like a knife, barely creating a splash. Regan hears cheers. A perfect dive.

He takes a deep breath and lets go of the rail. *Just walk out there and do it.* He edges outward. But he forgets his resolve not to and looks down at the rectangle of blue and the faces staring up at him like discs. The discs go all blurry, his legs tremble, he feels like he's going to throw up. Or pass out. His knees buckle. He turns back and lunges for the support of the rail.

"Geez, all you had to do was one lousy dive." Matt has found him in the change room, where he fled. "Why didn't you do it?"

He'll never forget that climb down, every step taking him closer to the group watching from below – like descending into hell, his own personal hell. He stepped onto the deck on wobbly legs, brushed past a sneering Nick, caught the amused looks on the other faces, and just kept going.

He doesn't try to explain – Matt wouldn't understand anyway. He pulls on his pants and shirt without waiting to dry himself, avoiding Matt's scathing look. The sooner he's out of here, the better. *I'll never come back.*

"What are you going to do when we're on that boat in the Caribbean?" There's contempt in Matt's voice. "Climb down the ladder like my grandmother every time you go for a swim?"

Regan heads for the door. Matt's voice follows him. "It was your chance to show them you had some guts."

At the door he bumps into Anthony. "Hey, wait up. I'll walk with you," Anthony says, as if nothing at all has happened. Regan doesn't really want company, but he's so surprised, he finds himself agreeing to wait. As the door swings shut, he hears Matt say, "What d'you want to walk with him for?" He doesn't catch Anthony's answer, but it sounds like he's giving Matt a hard time.

Outside in the corridor he leans against the wall, half-hidden by the Coke machine, hoping no one else he knows will come by. On the opposite wall is the list of rules: NO RUNNING ON DECK, NO HORSEPLAY, CAPS MANDATORY FOR LONG HAIR, SHOWER BEFORE ENTER-ING POOL, NO GLASS OR GUM, NO RADIOS, NO EATING NEAR POOL.

The door to the girls' change room opens and his sister, Carol, waltzes out. She's in her new sapphire blue Speedo, bought especially for their trip. When she sees him, she stops and glares. "Nice going, Regan."

"What?" he protests.

"Don't pretend you don't know."

He sighs. "Who told *you?*"

"Just about everyone," she says. "You should've known better than to climb up there in the first place."

He can't stomach another lecture right now. "I suppose *you* never make a mistake," he snaps.

She snaps right back. "At least I don't get talked into making an ass of myself in front of everyone. Wait'll Dad hears about this one."

Regan turns on his heels and heads for the door. He isn't going to hang around for anyone. Not even for Anthony.

"Wait —" Carol begins, her tone softening. But he's already out the door. She shrugs and goes to join her friends waiting poolside to admire her new Speedo.

2

Ah! well-a-day! what evil looks
Had I from old and young!
Instead of the cross, the Albatross
About my neck was hung.

Lanky, long-legged Anthony catches up to him before he's gone two blocks. "Hey, slow down. What's the rush?"

Regan stops. He feels he owes him an explanation. "I had to get away from that place."

"Yeah, I guess." They walk on in silence for a moment before Anthony speaks again. "Look, it's none of my business, but don't let those guys bug you, specially that Nick."

"Easy to say."

They wait for a bus to go by, then cross the street. "I know. But it happens. Happened to me once, back in the village where I grew up." Anthony goes on to tell how the guys he hung out with took turns lifting stuff from the general store on a dare and sharing it around – small stuff: chocolate bars, gum, comic books. More to show they had the nerve than anything else. But Anthony liked old Mr. Bennett, who ran the store, and he wouldn't do it when his turn came. The guys dissed him, accused him of being a wimp. It was a long time before they let him forget it. "Yeah, I know what it's like," he tells Regan.

Not quite the same thing, Regan thinks. *You knew you weren't a wimp — that wasn't the reason you wouldn't do it.* Still, he knows it would have been easier for Anthony just to play along with Nick and the others, especially when he's the new kid on the block. Yet he didn't. Regan decides he really likes Anthony.

It's partly because of Anthony that they were going to the Caribbean in the first place. Anthony's family had come to Canada a year ago, and he'd been in the same grade eight class as Regan and Matt. One day Anthony heard Matt talking in the locker room about sailing in a race on Lake Ontario with his father. "You'd really like sailing in the Caribbean," he'd told Matt. "And the best sailing in the whole Caribbean is in the Grenadines, where I come from. Best in the world, some say." Matt hadn't appeared to pay much attention, but when he'd heard his mother and father talking about chartering a sailboat somewhere exotic this summer, he remembered what Anthony had said.

One thing led to another and the next Regan heard, it was all arranged. Not without lots of grumbling from Regan's father about the cost and how it was all right for

Matt's father, who was a college professor, but why did *they* have to spend their money and their two week holiday on some fancy boat in the Caribbean?

"And besides, what do we know about sailing?" his father griped at the dinner table. "Different for them. They've been sailing for years."

"Yes, and aren't we lucky to have experienced sailors to go with?" Regan's mother said brightly.

They go through this every year, Regan thought, *like a ritual, slightly different each time but with the same ending.*

Mr. Lasker's pencil-thin mustache twitched in irritation. "But the cost!"

Mrs. Lasker smoothed the tablecloth with her hand. "Summer is the off-season down there. It's very reasonable to charter a boat, especially when two families are sharing the expense."

Regan pushed his brussels sprouts under a lettuce leaf to hide them, then speared the last piece of meat loaf on his plate. Sometimes it seemed that his mother and father were carrying on separate conversations, as if they were each talking to someone else.

His father tried another tack. "That miserable boss of mine will find some reason why I can't have my holidays in July."

"You have seniority," his mother said blithely. "You can insist on it."

At which his father changed the subject – the sign, Regan knew, that he was giving in. His mother had prevailed again. They would go on holidays with her sister and her husband, Regan's Aunt Shelley and Uncle Ron. And with their son, Matt.

Even so, he was excited then about sailing in the Grenadines. He pictured a long, pointed bow slicing through the sea, his feet planted on the foredeck, eyes shaded, sighting a thin blue smudge of land on the horizon and calling, "Land-ho!" Now, after what happened today at the pool, he has a different picture — twenty-four hours a day on a boat with Matt, who has just found him out. Found out what a wimp he is.

He tries to look on the bright side. Anthony will be there, back visiting his relatives for the summer. One good friend anyway.

They turn a corner and Regan realizes Anthony is talking to him. "It's great you guys are coming to the Grenadines," he's saying.

Regan watches a pair of crows on the road busily scavenging a dead squirrel as a truck bears down on them. *What they won't risk to get something to eat,* he thinks. *Food is life and death with them.*

"How much sailing have you done anyway?" Anthony asks casually.

"None," Regan admits. "You?"

"Been in boats since I was a little kid — mostly motor boats though. My grandfather used to be a fisherman, and he often took me with him. Just a small boat with an outboard, but we'd go way out – out of sight of land sometimes."

"Wow!" Regan wonders what it would be like to see nothing but ocean all the way to the horizon. *Scary,* he thinks. "Did you ever get lost?"

"Naw, Grandpa always knew exactly where we were. One of his brothers did though. Never came back. That was before I was born. Grandpa still talks about it."

"He never came back!"

Anthony nods grimly. "They figured his outboard must've stalled and he got blown west. That's what happens in the Caribbean if something goes wrong. The trade winds only blow one way, so you just keep goin' west – a thousand miles before you hit Central America. If you don't get swamped by a wave first, or die of thirst, or starve."

Pictures of a drifting boat with only a skeleton aboard flash through Regan's mind. "Couldn't your grandfather rescue him?"

"He tried. All his friends tried. They went out every day and searched. But it's tough to find a small boat in all that ocean. They kept searching for weeks and weeks, but they had to give up in the end. Maybe the sharks got him."

"There's *sharks!*"

"Oh, sure. Sometimes they'd come around when Grandpa and I were fishing late in the day. If they got too close, he'd bash them on the nose – that's their tender spot."

Regan blanches. He pictures a gaping jaw, rows of teeth pursuing him, closing on his leg.

Anthony, he learns, is leaving the next day. He'll be there ahead of them. "Grandpa sent me the money to come back and visit him," Anthony says. "My grandpa's a great guy."

"Will I be able to find you?" Regan asks.

"Oh, sure. It's small there. Everybody knows everybody. Not like here. I'll be with Grandpa most of the time. Just ask for Nathan Waterman. He has a business now, Nate's Marine. Fixes engines and stuff. Look for his boat – a blue cruiser."

When Regan gets home, his mother is busy making lists and sorting clothes to take with them. "I've a million things to do before next week," she tells him. "You can go to the drugstore for me, Regan."

He looks at the list his mother hands him: GRAVOL, SOLARCAINE, KAOPECTATE, TYLENOL, BAND-AIDS (large box), IODINE, SWIMMER'S EAR, BUG OFF (3 cans).

By the time he gets back, Carol is home. She's on the floor sorting through a huge pile of CDs. "They'd better have a decent stereo on that boat," she says, "or I'll go bonkers with only you two guys around." She spots the bag he's brought from the drugstore, looks through it. "Where's the extra shampoo and conditioner? Salt water makes a mess of my hair. Body lotion, too – can't live without body lotion. And hair spray. And geez, Regan, why didn't you get more sunblock?"

Regan ignores her and heads for the stairs. He wants to get back to the book he was reading. The one about the shipwrecked sailor – a true story. Kept him awake half the night imagining what it must have been like. He's not sure why he keeps reading, it makes him so jumpy. But once he got started, he couldn't stop. He has to find out what happens.

Carol looks up. "Thought you'd be out cutting the grass by now."

Regan pauses, one foot on the stairs. "I'm busy." He isn't going to let Carol know he's forgotten.

But she can read his mind, just by looking at him. "Forgot, didn't you? You're asking for trouble. You heard what Dad said."

He's blocked that out too. His mind tends to shut down when his father yells at him. "I'll do it tomorrow."

Carol chooses one last CD and adds it to the pile. She stands up and stretches. "In that case, I'll be sure to be back in time to enjoy the fireworks when Dad gets home."

Regan goes upstairs, closes the door of his room, and picks up his book. The picture on the cover shows an emaciated, sunburnt man in a life raft on an empty ocean. He's sighting with a makeshift sextant, trying to figure out where he is. "A sailor's story," the blurb says, "an amazing feat of survival at sea."

He flops onto the bed with the book. It's a good thing he reads fast – after this one, there are four more sea books he found at the library. One on snorkeling, one on reef fish of the Caribbean, one on basic sailing, and one on storm sailing. Oh, yeah, and one more he'd forgotten about, an old poem – *The Rime of the Ancient Mariner*. He isn't sure whether he'll get to that one. If he tries to take all those books with him, Carol will make some crack in front of everyone. The bookworm, she'll call him, or the book nerd.

He opens the sailor's story to where he left off – it's blowing a gale and the mounting waves are threatening to overturn his life raft. Regan shivers, reads gamely on. As he reads, his imagination is working overtime. This yacht they're chartering, what if it hits something and sinks? What if? . . .

He hears the front door slam and goes to the window to check. Carol is halfway down the block. Tossing the book onto the bed, he hurries downstairs and out the door. The story will have to wait. Now that Carol's left, he can cut the grass – he'd better before his father gets home, or else.

He struggles to push the mower through a thick patch, digging in his toes to keep it moving. His father refuses to spend the money for a power mower.

"But, Dad," Regan had said, "it's so old and everybody uses power mowers these days."

"I don't care what everybody does," his father said. "That's the mower I had to use when I was your age, and you can too."

"That was different," Regan argued. "There weren't any power mowers back then."

His father almost smiled. "How old do you think I am, anyway?" Then his stern look came back. "Of course there were power mowers then, but your grandfather liked doing things his way. And believe me, I wouldn't have dared argue back the way you do."

I hardly ever do, Regan wanted to say, but he didn't.

On *his* way home, Anthony is thinking about the Caribbean too. Mostly about how much he misses it; how he misses walking down the street and knowing everybody he meets. "Hey there, Tony," they'd say, or, "All right?" or, if it was one of his uncles or aunts, "How's your mother, Anthony?" though they'd probably seen her themselves the day before. Or, if it was the minister, "See you in church on Sunday, Anthony." Maybe just a nod from some, but always a sign they knew who he was, that he had a place in their world, that he wasn't a nobody.

Here people pass without even looking at you. Or, if they do, they just glance as you approach, then quickly look away again. Even those he sees every day, day after day, on his way to school – the mailman, the woman who's always in her yard gardening, the old guy who rocks on his front porch all day. None of them speak to him.

What can you expect, he tells himself, *they don't know me from Adam.* But it's more than that. . . . Sometimes he can feel the tension. Not that most aren't polite and everything – the store clerks, the teachers, the baseball coach, the other kids. All bending over backwards to show they aren't racist. But the tension's there just the same. Even in his class, it's there. And he sure isn't one of the guys yet.

Anyway, he thinks, *I'll be back in the Islands soon. In just a few days. Thanks to Grandpa. When Regan gets there, I can show him around, get together with some of the guys I used to hang out with. Then again, maybe Regan won't go for that, maybe he'll feel the way I do up here — different from everyone around him. And Regan won't be used to it like I am, might not be able to handle it. Better to just meet up with him on their boat. Maybe Grandpa and I can help them a little. Let them know some of the things to watch out for.*

Suppose down there I'll be boastin' to everyone about how great things are up in Canada — like up here, I boast about the Grenadines. Wish I could carry a bunch of snowballs in my pack. Have a snowball fight with the guys down there. They wouldn't believe it — snow up to your knees. Just like people here wouldn't believe how a storm can turn the sweet blue Caribbean into a monster, or how many reefs there are waiting to catch your boat when you're not lookin', or how much power there is in those swells that have been building all the way from Africa.

3

It is an ancient Mariner
And he stoppeth one of three. . . .
He holds him with his skinny hand,
'There was a ship,' quoth he.

When the flight lands at St. Vincent in the Grenadines, Carol's first out the door and down the steps. Regan, who can't bring himself to push his way into the line the way his sister does, emerges at the end. Waves of heat rising from the asphalt tarmac hit him, and the brightness makes him squint as he follows the others to the small, open airport.

The back of his father's shirt is already wet with sweat. "*Phew,* is it always this hot?" his father grumbles.

"Summer in the Tropics," Matt's father says. "It'll be cooler on the water."

I'm just glad we're here, Regan thinks.

He'd been apprehensive enough about his first trip in a plane, then his mother had selected a seat for him between Matt and Carol. *Probably thinks she's doing me a favor,* he told himself. *Some favor!* It was the first time he'd seen Matt since that day at the pool, and when they gathered at the Toronto airport, Matt hardly looked at him. Regan began to feel as if he were invisible.

On the plane, he had an urge to talk to calm his nerves. "Wonder if they'll give us a meal?" he asked, just for something to say. Matt merely shrugged. "How high do these things fly anyway?" he tried next, although he really didn't want to know. Matt buried his nose deeper in *Sports Illustrated* and Regan gave up.

Next to him, Carol had the window seat. At least they hadn't put him there, he'd thought, where he couldn't help looking down ten or twenty thousand feet and imagining the plane in a death spiral.

Trapped between the two of them, he'd dug out his library books. He'd already finished the sailor's story and the snorkeling book. He didn't want Matt to see him reading *Basic Sailing,* so he opened the other one, the one called *Heavy Weather Sailing.*

Heavy weather, he soon discovered, meant when the waves were about the size of buildings. The photographs alone were terrifying. He turned to the chapter about the annual Fastnet Yacht Race, from England to Ireland around Land's End, when they encountered a Force 11 gale, almost a hurricane. Yachts were overturned, masts ripped off, five boats and fifteen crewmen were lost. He was staring transfixed at a photograph of a capsized yacht when he realized someone was leaning across him. It was Carol, trying to get Matt's attention.

"Hey, Matt." She had to talk loudly over the noise of the engines. "How many bedrooms are there on this boat?"

Matt looked up from his magazine. "Cabins," he said.

"What?"

"They're called cabins, not bedrooms."

"Whatever. How many?"

They were talking back and forth across Regan as if he weren't there. He felt like a spectator at a tennis match.

"Two doubles and a single probably," Matt said. "She's a big boat. A forty-two footer."

Carol looked relieved. "Good. I'll take the single. Hope it has a lock on the door and its own bathroom."

Matt gave her a withering look. "Head. They're called heads, not bathrooms."

Regan had been doing a calculation of his own. "So where do you and I sleep then?" he asked Matt. "Our parents will want the two doubles."

Matt shrugged. "Anywhere we want, I guess – the cockpit, the saloon. What's it matter?"

The saloon? Regan thought a saloon was a dance hall in the old West but he didn't ask. He remembered there was a list of sailing terms in the back of his *Basic Sailing* book. He snuck a look at it and found lots of peculiar words, like "clew" and "leech" and "spinnaker" and "backstay," but no "saloon." Well, he guessed he'd find out soon enough if he had to sleep in one.

Now the long plane ride is over. They're here, actually here in the Caribbean, and they're going to live on a yacht! And Anthony is here too. He begins to think the next week may be all right – so long as they don't encounter waves like the ones in that *Heavy Weather Sailing* book. He's nervous about the barracuda too, the ones he read about in the snorkeling book. The book claimed they don't usually attack swimmers, but that word "usually" bothers him.

They wait for their luggage, a silent sweating group. A local family beside them greets arriving relatives with hugs and whoops of welcome. Regan watches them and hopes he'll meet up with Anthony soon. He'll have to keep his eyes peeled for a blue cruiser.

The customs man waves them through after a quick look at their bags. Outside, a van is waiting to take them to the marina, along with a couple who are also chartering a boat.

"Have you sailed here before?" Matt's father asks the couple.

"Many times," the woman says. "It's a great place to sail."

"Always a good breeze – the trade winds, you know," the man adds. "Lot of reefs though. You have to keep a sharp lookout for them."

That's what Anthony said too, thinks Regan.

They drive through a village where men in white shirts and pants are playing cricket in a field. Women sing as they wash clothes in a stream. The modest houses are colorfully painted – pink, yellow, blue, even purple – and the windows have shutters instead of glass. Regan's mother points to a bush loaded with bright red flowers and sniffs the perfumed air. "Look at that! Hibiscus growing wild!"

Farther on, the stout woman driver stops by the roadside to show them a banana grove. "Funny to see a tree full of bananas," Regan says to Matt. Matt snaps his gum.

"You have to study the charts carefully," the couple are saying. "But if in doubt, you can tell where the reefs are by the color of the water."

Regan wants to ask how, but at that moment they come over a hill and catch sight of a whole forest of masts. The blue water of the Caribbean sparkles beyond.

"The marina," the driver says.

Beside Regan, Matt suddenly comes to life. "Wow, look at all those boats!" As soon as the van stops, he and Regan pile out and race down the hill toward the docks.

"There are bags to carry, boys!" Matt's father calls after them. Regan stops and watches a man with a beltful of tools being hauled to the top of a mast in a bosun's chair. The mast sways as a wave rocks the boat and he's glad he's not the one up there. He turns and follows Matt back up the hill.

The marina office is jammed with charts and sailing gear, and the walls are covered with maps and pictures of boats. The manager is on the phone. In the background a VHF radio crackles and a voice says, "This is *Serenader* calling *Happy Days*. *Serenader* calling *Happy Days*. Over."

Regan wanders over to a large map of the West Indies on the wall. It shows a whole string of small islands running in an arc from the Virgin Islands in the north to Trinidad in the south. He finds St. Vincent and the Grenadines toward the southern end of the chain. *Wow,* he thinks, *we're almost all the way to South America!*

The manager hangs up and comes over to greet them. "Your boat is on C Dock, slip twenty-eight," he says. "You'll find charts on board for the whole area." He asks who the captain is and Matt's father says he guesses he's been elected.

"Oh, yes, you must be Mr. O'Brien," the manager says. "I remember you saying in your letter you'd sailed for years on Lake Ontario. I know you're very experienced, but it can be tricky sailing down here if you've never been before. I'll be happy to go over the charts with you and answer any questions." Matt's father says maybe later, after he's had a chance to look over the boat, and they set off.

As the others file out of the office, Regan hangs back. "Do you know a Mr. Waterman, sir?"

"Nathan Waterman?" the manager says. "Sure, everybody knows Nate."

"His grandson, Anthony, is a friend of mine from school," Regan explains. "Can you tell me where I'd find him?"

"As a matter of fact, I heard Nate on the VHF this morning," the manager tells him. "A boat with an engine problem was calling him to come over to Bequia." He pronounces it Beckwee. "If your folks are planning to sail there, you'll probably find Anthony with him."

Regan thanks him and hurries out the door to catch up with the others.

They march along the dock with their luggage, past rows of yachts. Luxurious motor cruisers loaded with chrome, and all sorts of sailboats – sleek modern sloops with one mast, ketches with two masts, even a few old schooners with wooden masts. At one dock is a line of charter boats belonging to the marina, at the other docks, cruising boats with flags from all over the world – some empty, some with their owners varnishing woodwork or polishing brass.

"I've never seen so many big sailboats!" Matt says. "Makes our marina back home look pretty pathetic."

At least he's talking to me, Regan thinks. *That's a good sign.*

At slip twenty-eight, a sloop with a gleaming golden yellow hull and shiny steel vents on the cabin top sits quietly waiting for them. ARCTURUS it says, in big letters on the bow. Regan stares, wide-eyed. *Arcturus!* He's heard that name before somewhere. *Of course, the star!*

They climb aboard and set the bags down in the cockpit. Matt's father gives a long low whistle as he gazes around. "She's a beauty!"

Regan wonders if he'll ever figure out the maze of lines and strange-looking mechanisms on the deck. His mother must be thinking the same thing. "You'll have to explain everything to us, Ron," she says, with a nervous laugh. "We're novices, you know."

"You'll be fine," Matt's father says. "Don't worry." They follow him down five steep steps leading below. "This is called the companionway," he says.

At the bottom, Regan stops in amazement, for in front of him is a complete house. A living/dining room with a sofa on one side and a U-shaped bench and table on the other – but it's different than the usual living room: a sturdy aluminum mast extends up through the middle of it. A kitchen, two bathrooms, and three bedrooms – or rather, two heads and three cabins he remembers to call them – plus a desk with a bunch of dials above it, which, he learns, is the navigation station. *How could it all have been squeezed into such a small space?* he wonders.

He decides he'd better listen, as his Uncle Ron is explaining what things are called. The living/dining room is the saloon. *So that's the saloon.* The kitchen is the galley. "Even the floor has a special name," Uncle Ron says. "It's called the sole. Best to call things by their nautical names or people will think you're a landlubber."

Regan's parents put their bags in the big cabin near the bow, and Carol takes possession of the small one beside it. Matt's parents take the stern cabin to be near the cockpit. Matt's father points to the sofa, which he calls the settee. "You two boys can share that," he says. "It pulls out to make a double bed."

Matt makes a face. "Think I'll sleep in the cockpit, Dad," he says.

Suddenly, they all stagger and grab for support as *Arcturus* rocks violently. Regan, who happens to be in the galley, grabs the stove, but it swings away from him and he ends up sprawled on the floor. He jumps up, embarrassed. "Hey, the stove moved!"

"You okay, Regan?" his mother asks.

"Yeah, but why did it do that?"

"It's on gimbals," Uncle Ron explains. "So it'll stay level, and the pots and pans won't slide off when the boat heels."

Heels! Gimbals! Regan realizes he still has a lot to learn if he isn't to talk like a landlubber. Anthony won't talk like one. Well, he won't either.

When *Arcturus* settles down again, Uncle Ron looks out. "Ferry went by and made some waves, that's all. Matt, you and Regan go up top and put out a couple more fenders in case we bump the dock. And check the dinghy," he calls after them.

Matt opens a locker and hauls out two round rubber things, like giant white sausages. He lowers these between the side of the boat and the dock, and ties them to the boat's lifelines. Then they go to the stern and look at the dinghy drifting quietly on its line behind *Arcturus. Like a colt holding on to its mother's tail,* Regan thinks. It's a gray inflatable dinghy, with a shiny out-board on the stern and the name DISCOVERY in black letters on the bow.

"Neat dinghy!" Regan says. "Think we'll get to drive it?"

"I can," Matt says. "I drive our dinghy all the time at home. But you can't until Dad checks you out." He peers at the outboard. "It's a fifteen horse. That oughta go some."

He's almost being friendly, Regan thinks. But he knows it's only because he can't resist talking about boats. Every time Matt looks at him, Regan figures he still sees a trembling wimp climbing down from the diving tower and slinking away.

Will Matt ever forget? he wonders. *Will I? Does something like that stay with you for the rest of your life, like it's hanging around your neck? Or can you somehow get past it?*

He wishes he knew the answer. Lost in thought, he doesn't notice the dinghy drift up and nudge the stern as if it's trying to get his attention. Unaware, he turns and follows Matt below. The dinghy drifts back to the end of its tether, biding its time, waiting. Waiting for its chance to help Regan answer his question.

4

The ship was cheered, the harbor cleared,
Merrily did we drop
Below the kirk, below the hill,
Below the lighthouse top.

"What are those called, Uncle Ron?" Regan points to two round shiny things, like oversized stainless steel spools, one on either side of the cockpit.

"Winches," his uncle says. "For pulling in the sheets."

Sheets? Regan looks around, but he can't see anything that looks like a sheet. His uncle holds up a rope with blue stripes that runs from the cockpit along the deck to the bow, where it's attached to a rolled-up sail. "This is a sheet," he says. "The jib sheet."

"Oh," Regan says, nodding. *So a sheet is a rope attached to a sail. And the jib must be that sail at the bow.* He sighs; he's learning but it's confusing sorting everything out. He's been following Matt and his father around the deck while they inspect the rigging. He's waiting for a chance to ask his uncle if they can sail to Bequia so he can find Anthony. Meantime he keeps hearing strange words, like "stays" and "travelers" and "halyards" and "shrouds." He's full of questions, but Matt rolls his eyes if he asks a dumb one. Like when he asked if the shrouds are what they wrap dead people in. Turns out the shrouds are the wires running from the mast to the deck to steady it. But how was he to know that?

Finally, Matt's father seems satisfied with his inspection and he and Matt go below to look at the charts and instruments at the navigation station. Regan trails along. He hears them mention Bequia. This is his chance.

"Can we sail there today, Uncle Ron?" he asks. "My friend Anthony's in Bequia and I'd really like to see him."

"We'll be going to Bequia, Regan, but not today," his uncle says. "Have to stock up on groceries first if we want to eat."

Regan's mother and Aunt Shelley are busy making a list. His father's gone to inquire about snorkeling gear. "We're off to the supermarket now," Regan's mother says. "You kids better come with us to help with the bags."

"I need Matt, if you don't mind," Matt's father says. "We'll finish up here, then we'll go over the charts with the marina manager."

Regan wishes he could stay too, but he knows he wouldn't be much help. He follows the others to the marina office, where they find a taxi waiting for a fare. "Supermarket? Sure ting," says the driver.

Singing along with his blaring radio, the driver

doesn't seem to notice the heat or the dust swirling in the open window. Regan sits beside him, sweltering, taking in the sights. He watches a group of uniformed school children, laughing and jostling together. A man by the side of the road is splitting coconuts with a machete and selling them to passersby. A sweet smell wafts in the window from a roadside stand shaded by a red and yellow umbrella. "Fried plantain," says the driver, sniffing appreciatively. "The best." A goat wanders across the road, paying no attention to the taxi's blaring horn.

Regan's surprised to see the supermarket isn't much different from the one at home. Smaller, maybe, but lots of fish and lots of fruit – huge stalks of bananas, one of which his mother plunks in the cart with wobbly wheels that Regan is pushing. At the checkout, he stares at the pretty cashier, with ribbons in her hair, until she stares back and makes him blush.

When they come out with their bags of groceries, a line of taxi drivers calls to them. They stand confused, not understanding a word of the rapid-fire West Indian patois. Eventually the driver who brought them claims them back amid much good-natured bantering from the others.

Back at the marina, with the trunk full of groceries, Regan and Carol have one of their tussling matches. This ones's over the marina's big-wheeled luggage cart and who will get to wheel it. Carol manages to shove Regan aside and races the cart loaded with groceries triumphantly along the dock to *Arcturus*.

She climbs aboard and Regan begins passing bags across to her, but one splits open midway. "Regan! Watch what you're doing!" Carol shrieks, as the whole huge stalk of bananas hits the water with a splash and drifts away. They start a shouting match over whose fault it was.

"Never mind that!" their mother calls from the dock. "Get the bananas!"

Their father rushes up from below. "What's going on?" They all stare at the bananas drifting away.

Matt and his father come along the dock. "Get the boat hook," Uncle Ron calls, pointing, and Regan jumps aboard, grabs it, and runs to the stern followed by Carol, who's trying to wrench the boat hook away from him. After a struggle, during which Regan almost falls in, he somehow manages to fish out the bananas.

He goes back to handing the remaining bags across, while Carol keeps reminding him to do it properly, with one hand on the bottom. *Bossy sister,* he thinks, *if only I was two years older than you instead of the other way around.* When the groceries are all stowed, he wanders up to the bow to get away.

Out on the bay, a boy is learning to windsurf. He watches as the boy falls off, climbs on again, sails a few yards, falls off, climbs on again, sails a few more yards, falls off. But he finally does manage to stay on, and Regan cheers him silently as he sails away.

After dinner, Uncle Ron unrolls a chart and spreads it out on the table, weighing it down with the salt and pepper and mustard. "Here's Bequia," he says, pointing to a small island to the south. "We'll sail there tomorrow, so let's get an early start. I want to arrive while there's still good light to see the reefs. And that will give us time to explore the island."

That night, Regan lies on the opened-up sofa, listening to the sound of a calypso band from somewhere across the bay. The reflection of the marina lights in the water makes shifting patterns on the ceiling above him, like a light show. *First time ever sleeping on a boat,* he thinks. He's glad they're still at the dock. Tomorrow they'll be out there with all those reefs and big waves and stuff. He can hear the water sloshing back and forth in the bilge beneath him, and he rolls over and stares down at the floor, er, sole. His uncle said there is always some water under there and not to worry; if the water level gets too high, the bilge pump will come on automatically and pump it out. *But what if the pump doesn't come on when it's supposed to? Will the water just keep on rising, right up to my bed? Will I wake up in time to get out, or will I be trapped down here?*

He tosses and turns, wondering if he'll lie awake all night in this strange bedroom. But the back-and-forth movement of the boat rocks him, the lights on the ceiling mesmerize him, the calypso music fades away, and before long he's sound asleep.

"Out of bed, Regan! We're late. How many times do I have to call you?"

He jerks upright, then slumps back and closes his eyes again. Through the open hatch he can hear Matt and his father in the cockpit, talking. Something about dock lines.

"You should be up there helping Matt," his father says. Regan sits up. He's surprised to see his father getting out plates and cutlery while his mother makes breakfast. Aunt Shelley is at the navigation station plotting their course on a chart. Carol can be heard splashing in the shower, though Uncle Ron had told them to go easy on the fresh water. "There's only so much in the tanks," he said. It doesn't seem to faze Carol. She likes long showers.

He throws on shorts and a T-shirt and climbs sleepily to the cockpit just as Uncle Ron turns the key and cranks the engine. "We're way behind schedule," he tells Regan. "Everyone slept in." The diesel roars throatily as he revs it. "We'll get under way while the others make breakfast. You can help Matt with the dock lines."

Matt sends Regan to uncleat the bow line while he handles the stern line. They walk the boat back, then jump aboard with the lines while Uncle Ron eases *Arcturus* out of the slip, shifts into forward, and heads for the channel leading out of the harbor.

They're off.

5

He prayeth best, who loveth best
All things both great and small;

Regan helps Matt coil the lines and take in the fenders. It's calm in the harbor and the boat slices through the quiet waters, but as soon as they round the point and head out, the wind hits them and the bow begins to pound into the waves. Suddenly there's a crash from below.

"Hey!" a voice yells. "The dishes!"

"Better secure everything down there," Matt's father calls, as they hammer into another big swell.

Clang! Crash! More noises from below.

"Take the wheel, Matt," his father says. "I'll raise the sails. It'll be smoother going with the sails up and the engine off." He makes his way forward on the pitching deck and begins untying the mainsail, which is wrapped neatly around the boom.

Regan watches Matt and his father working together as a team. They seem to know what to do without even talking. He envies Matt, braced behind the wheel. His father treats him like he isn't just a kid.

At a signal, Matt wheels the boat into the wind while his father cranks the main up. The big sail flaps violently, making such a racket Regan's sure something has gone wrong. The power of the wind startles him as the sail whips back and forth. But Matt's father ignores the wild flapping and calmly unfurls the jib as well. The jib adds to the din, cracking like a gun going off, while the sheets thrash about like snakes gone berserk.

His uncle jumps back in the cockpit, grabs one of the thrashing jib sheets, and shows Regan how to wrap it around the winch. "Always wrap it clockwise," he says. "Now crank it in." Regan cranks on the winch handle for all he's worth, slowly pulling in the flapping jib. "Keep going," his uncle tells him.

His arm muscles ache, but he keeps cranking. The jib quietens down and begins to fill with wind as the sheet pulls it in.

"Good work, Regan," Uncle Ron says.

He feels a surge of pride. He wishes his father had heard that.

While he's been working the winch, Matt has wheeled the bow off the wind. Both the jib and the main billow out, and *Arcturus* leaps ahead. Regan is jerked back by the sudden acceleration.

"Wow!" A thrill courses through him, from the top

of his head to the soles of his feet. Now the boat is heeling and charging through the waves. With the engine off, the only sounds are the hissing of the sea, rushing past the hull, and the creaking of lines and rigging. The bow settles to a steady up-and-down motion.

The others come up from below, bringing juice and eggs and toast. But the minute he looks at the food, Regan realizes something has happened to his insides. Something awful. He's been so excited, the squeamish feeling has crept up on him unnoticed. Now it hits. He sits down shakily on the cockpit bench, sure he's about to throw up in front of everyone.

Beside him Carol is wolfing down eggs and toast. She looks perfectly healthy. *She would be,* he thinks. He stares miserably at the sea ahead, trying hard to keep from vomiting. *If I do have to, where should I do it?* Suddenly he has no choice. He turns, leans over the rail, and lets go. It comes back − right in his face, and elsewhere.

"Yuck! All over my breakfast!" Carol shrieks. She flings plate and all over the side. "Gross!"

"He couldn't help it," her mother admonishes. She gently leads Regan below to wipe off his face and urges him to lie down.

But he'd rather be in the fresh air. He comes back up and takes gulps of it. With nothing left in his stomach, he feels a little better. His father, who's looking a little green himself, pats him on the shoulder sympathetically, then quickly drops his hand as if embarrassed by this display of emotion. Just one little pat − no more − but for some reason, it reminds Regan of a small boy sitting on his father's knee while his father reads the Sunday comics aloud. Regan on one knee, Carol on the other. *Did that really happen?*

"Just a word to the wise, in case anyone else feels seasick," his Aunt Shelley says. "It helps to look straight ahead instead of watching the water go by the side. And if you do have to throw up, do it to leeward, not windward. That way it won't come back at you."

Regan concentrates on staring straight ahead. Suddenly he sees something by the bow. It looks like a fin. He rubs his eyes. *Am I hallucinating? No, there's another, and another!*

He leaps up, seasickness temporarily forgotten. "Hey! Sharks!"

Everyone rushes to the side to look. Three sleek bodies arch gracefully out of the sea and back in again. "They're dolphins, not sharks," Matt's father says. He relieves Matt at the wheel so he can go and look at them, and Regan and Carol follow Matt onto the foredeck. "Hang on up there, you kids," Matt's father calls.

Regan grabs the lifelines and works his way forward behind Matt. He can see the three dolphins just under the surface, racing alongside the bow, easily keeping up with the boat. Their slick, shiny, streamlined bodies arch in and out of the water, and he can hear clicking sounds and a sort of singsong noise. *They're talking to each other,* he thinks, *maybe talking about us. Who are these strange creatures who live in the air?* he imagines them saying. The smallest dolphin rolls on its side and stares up at him with one eye. As they gaze at each other, Regan is struck with wonder. He's seen lots of dolphins on TV, but this is different. This is a real live dolphin in the wild.

A brave little guy, he thinks. He wouldn't want to live down there, with sharks and killer whales and who knows what else, just waiting for him to make a mistake so he can become their next meal. The trio stay with the boat for miles, playing in the bow wave. Then, as suddenly as they came, they disappear.

Regan follows Matt and Carol back to the cockpit and slumps down, his nausea returning. He can't believe his luck when his uncle motions to him. "Steering's the best thing for seasickness," his uncle says quietly.

Eagerly, Regan takes up a stance by his uncle at the wheel. "It's not like steering a bicycle or a car," Uncle Ron tells him. "There's no road to follow; you find your way by watching the compass. See what it reads now?"

Regan peers at the compass, floating in a stand in front of the wheel. "Looks like 200 degrees," he guesses. He thinks back to his Boy Scout training. "That's a little west of south, isn't it?"

"Right. Due south is 180 degrees. Now see what happens when I turn to port – that's left." Uncle Ron turns the wheel slightly to the left and the compass swings from 200 to 195, then to 190 degrees. "Now we're off course, so I have to correct." He turns the wheel slightly to the right and the compass swings back to 200 degrees. "Get the idea?"

Suddenly he lets go of the wheel. "All yours then, Regan. Keep her there."

Startled, Regan grips the wheel tightly. He stares at the compass. The others are watching him now, his father looking uneasy. The compass wanders and Regan jerks the wheel to correct. *Too far!* He jerks it back. *Too far the other way!* The compass swings wildly and the sails begin to flap. *What do I do now?* Regan wonders, in a panic.

"Whoa! Easy does it," his uncle says. "Just a bit at a time." And gradually he begins to get the hang of it, and the compass settles down. He finds that the bow has a tendency to yaw from side to side as they are sailing downwind on what his uncle calls a broad reach. The boat rolls a bit as well. He learns how to handle that, but he gets nervous if his uncle moves too far away.

A sloop going in the opposite direction passes and the helmsman waves at Regan. He waves back from behind the wheel. *Just one sailor to another,* he thinks proudly. But then, his attention wandering, he lets the bow veer – the sails make a racket and the main boom suddenly swings toward him. "Duck!" Uncle Ron shouts. He ducks and the heavy boom rattles by, just missing his head.

His uncle grabs the wheel to help him get back on course, while his aunt quickly sheets in the main. The boom comes swinging back and settles down where it was. "That was a jibe," Uncle Ron says. "It happens when the wind is behind you and switches from one side of the sail to the other. That pushes the boom over to the other side of the boat."

"Sure wouldn't want to get hit on the head with that boom when it's going by," Regan's father says.

"An accidental jibe can be dangerous," Aunt Shelley agrees. "But sometimes you jibe on purpose; then it's okay because you expect it."

Shaken, Regan pays close attention from then on. He stares hard at the compass, determined to keep on course. He also watches the sails, alert to any wind shift that may cause them to flutter.

After a while, Uncle Ron unrolls the chart and studies it. "There's a big reef at the entrance to Bequia harbor," he says. "It's called the Devil's Table. I'll take over before we get to that."

Regan certainly hopes so. The last thing he wants to do now is get mixed up with a reef. Especially one called the Devil's Table.

6

The harbor-bay was clear as glass,
So smoothly it was strewn!

It's midafternoon by the time they reach Bequia. They skirt the north shore, along the headland that marks the entrance to the harbor. As they approach, gusts of wind blast down from the headland, heeling *Arcturus* sharply, and swells threaten to push them onto the Devil's Table. Regan watches anxiously, but Uncle Ron has the wheel now and they barrel past the reef and tack into the harbor.

The harbor itself is calm and still. *Like a different world from out there,* Regan thinks.

"We'll lower the sails and motor in from here," his uncle says.

Carol decides she wants to get into this sailing too and she helps Matt drop the main while Regan rolls up the jib. Uncle Ron starts the engine and motors through a crowd of boats at anchor. One is a blue motor cruiser.

Could be Anthony's grandfather's boat, Regan thinks, but he sees no sign of anyone on board.

Uncle Ron circles, looking for room to anchor, watching the depth gauge. Seems to Regan there's lots of places, but they keep circling. "Have to find a spot where we won't swing into another boat if there's a wind shift in the night," his uncle explains. "Never know which way you'll end up facing, and I sure don't want to have to move in the middle of the night." Finally he picks out a spot in front of a red ketch and shifts into neutral. *Arcturus* glides slowly to a stop.

At the bow, Matt stands by the anchor, Regan beside him watching. When his father signals, Matt tilts the anchor overboard.

Regan jumps back, startled, as fifty feet of anchor chain roar through the chock, dragged by the weight of the plunging anchor. It hits bottom and *Arcturus* drifts back while Matt pays out more chain, then some of the line attached to the chain. He cleats the line and they go back to the cockpit to coil the sheets and furl the mainsail for the night.

"We've got the rest of the day in Bequia," Matt's father says. "Then, tomorrow, we'll head out for here." On the chart he points to a small group of islands farther south.

"Tobago . . ." Carol reads, squinting at the chart. "Tobago. . . Cays?" She says "cays" as if it rhymes with gays.

"It's pronounced keys, like in car keys, Carol," Regan says. He gets a dirty look for correcting her. "Anthony told me about Tobago Cays," he goes on, undeterred. "Says it's the best snorkeling in the Grenadines." He asks his uncle if he and Matt can take the dinghy over to the blue cruiser to look for his friend.

"Ever run an outboard, Regan?" his uncle wants to know.

"No, but I'd like to learn."

"I'll give you a quick lesson then."

"Me, too!" Carol chimes in, and she jumps in the dinghy before Regan can move. "What do I do first?"

"Make sure it's in neutral," Uncle Ron says. "That's very important." He shows her how to shift the gear lever into neutral. "Now set the handle at START, and pull. If it doesn't start after a few pulls, squeeze this little bulb to pump up more gas."

Carol pulls. Nothing happens. She squeezes the bulb and pulls again. Still nothing.

"Harder," Uncle Ron says, and she yanks harder. The motor starts with a roar. She practices starting and revving the motor over and over again, while Regan waits impatiently.

"Okay, Regan's turn," his uncle says finally. "Shut it off now, Carol."

Regan and Carol change places. "Bet you don't do it right," she taunts as they pass.

He carefully sets the handle at START, braces himself, and gives a mighty tug. The motor thunders into life. And the dinghy leaps forward! It bounces off the stern of *Arcturus*. The motor stalls.

Shaken, Regan stares at the motor. "Why'd it do that?"

"Apparently it wasn't in neutral, Regan," his uncle says. "That's the first thing to check, remember? Never start a motor in gear."

"But I thought Carol left it in neutral," Regan protests.

His uncle shakes his head. "Always check. No matter what you think. It must have been in gear because it took off as soon as you started it. Lucky the motor stalled. Anyway, it was a good lesson. Better let Matt drive over. You can practice on the way back."

When Matt's father has gone below, Regan glares at Carol. "You left it in gear on purpose, didn't you?"

"You were supposed to check," Carol shoots back.

"Just get out of the dinghy, Carol!"

"Make me. It's not your dinghy."

Regan's temper flares. He gives her a shove. She shoves back and he almost tumbles overboard.

"Hey!" Matt says. "Cut it out, you guys, or you'll both end up in the water."

"He will for sure," Carol says.

"Don't be long, you kids," their mother calls up from below. "We want to go ashore and look around."

Matt drives, perched on the rounded side. Regan and Carol, not speaking, share the seat that straddles the middle of the dinghy. When a wave from a passing boat rocks them, Regan clutches the side so he won't slide over. The last thing he wants to do is touch his sister.

Matt weaves skillfully in and out through the many anchored boats. "There it is," Regan says, pointing to the blue cruiser.

As they approach, Matt cuts the motor, glides neatly alongside, and grabs the cruiser's toe rail. "Ahoy! Anyone on board?"

Silence. Regan tries. "You there, Anthony?" When there's no answer, he takes hold of the lifeline and hoists himself up.

"Wait!" Matt says, sharply.

Regan pauses, one foot on the cruiser rail, one on the side of the dinghy. "Why?"

"You have to ask before you board someone else's boat. It's the law of the sea. 'Permission to board,' that's what you ask."

"But what if there's no one to ask?"

"Then you can't board. You wouldn't go into someone's house if they didn't answer the door, would you?"

Regan stubbornly stays half in and half out, looking around the cruiser's cockpit. He spots something familiar.

"Sit down, dummy – you heard what Matt said," Carol orders. "This is a waste of time, anyway. Could be anybody's boat."

But Regan's seen what he was looking for. He gets back in the dinghy, smiling. "It's Anthony's boat all right," he tells them. "I saw his Blue Jays cap in the cockpit."

"Lots of those around," Matt scoffs. "Who cares

about finding Anthony, anyway?" He changes places with Regan. "Your turn to drive – if you can."

This time Regan makes sure the motor's in neutral. He gives a mighty yank; the motor catches. "First pull!" he yelps.

Carol rolls her eyes. "Big deal."

Their parents are waiting in the cockpit when they get back. Regan aims the dinghy carefully, hoping to glide smoothly alongside, like Matt did at the blue cruiser. He cuts the motor. The dinghy stops dead a good ten feet short of *Arcturus*.

"Nice landing," Carol says. Regan sits there feeling foolish, while Matt, after two attempts, manages to throw the bow line to his father, who hauls them in.

With all seven of them packed in, the dinghy's low in the water, but it's only a short distance to the dinghy dock. The small dock is jammed, but they manage to squeeze in and tie up.

They follow a well-trodden path along a palm-lined beach. The path fronts a string of shops facing the harbor – an open-air restaurant, a pizza parlor, an ice-cream shop, a hotel with a red roof, and stores with displays of brightly colored clothes, model whaling boats, and rope hammocks. Vendors, some sporting dreadlocks, offer T-shirts, rope work, paintings of seascapes. Local boys hold up hand-carved model sailboats for sale, each assuring passersby that his model will sail the fastest.

Passing Mac's Pizzeria, a tantalizing aroma stops them. "How about a pizza, Mom?" Carol asks.

"Maybe later," her mother says. "When we're ready to go back." She's peering in a shop displaying local pottery and paintings. "This place looks interesting. Let's go in."

"Yes, let's," Aunt Shelley agrees.

Carol kicks at the ground. "Can I go practice driving the dinghy instead, Mom? Just around the harbor."

Her mother looks at Matt's father questioningly. He shrugs. "I guess that'd be all right. But stay inside the harbor. And Matt will have to go with you."

"Okay, Matt?" Carol asks.

"Better than shopping," Matt says.

"Come back in an hour to pick us up," her mother instructs.

"At the dinghy dock," her father adds. "And don't be late."

Carol races back to the dinghy, followed by Matt. With a choice of trailing around after the adults or riding in the dinghy, Regan decides to go too.

Carol starts the motor. "First, put it in reverse and back out," Matt tells her. She does, turning the motor to steer as she backs. But she also turns the throttle up by mistake. The dinghy shoots backward toward the beach.

"Put it in forward!" Matt shouts.

Carol shoves the gear to forward. The dinghy charges back toward the dock. A group of tourists on the shore stop to watch.

"No, that way, that way!" Matt waves his arm.

"Watch out!" Regan shouts. He scrambles to the bow and tries to hold them off, but they barrel ahead, pushing other dinghies aside.

"Shut it off!" Matt yells.

"Make up your mind!" Carol snaps.

The motor dies. The jumble of dinghies calms down, like a flock of birds that has been stirred up. Regan wishes the tourists would stop staring and grinning at them.

Matt gets out an oar. He paddles until they are well clear of the dock before they try again.

"Why didn't you do that in the first place?" Carol says.

She starts the motor and they head out into harbor.

7

The Sun's rim dips; the stars rush out:
At one stride comes the dark;

They make a circuit of the harbor without further incident. Carol weaves in and out among the anchored boats, practicing turns. "This is easy," she says, ignoring the glares from the people aboard the boats as she skims past, just missing their anchor lines. She heads for the outer harbor. The calm waters turn rough there, and the dinghy is bounced by waves.

Regan ducks as a spray of salt water shoots over the bow. "We're supposed to stay in the harbor," he reminds his sister.

"Yeah, yeah, I know." At the outer reaches of the harbor, she points to a deserted stretch of sand. "Nice beach there. Let's land."

Matt frowns. "I don't know," he begins. "The surf . . ."

But Carol is already heading in. A wave picks up the

dinghy and gives it a mighty shove shoreward. It's too late to turn back now.

Regan tenses as they approach. "Cut the motor!" Matt orders. "Now tilt it up," he shouts, as the prop guard scrapes the sand.

Motor tilted, the dinghy speeds toward the beach, propelled by the surf. It appears it will make a neat bow-first landing. Then, at the last moment, a wave shoves the dinghy sideways. Matt leaps into the knee-deep water, struggles to bring the bow back around, but successive waves toss the dinghy sideways onto the beach, then pull it out again, then hammer it in once more. Regan and Carol tumble out and join Matt. The dinghy bangs into them, sending them all down in a heap. Finally, they each grab one of the loops of rope running along the dinghy's side and manage to haul it up on the beach.

"*Whew!*" Matt says. "That surf's powerful! It almost flipped it over – would have ruined the motor."

Regan's legs feel weak. "You shouldn't have come in here, Carol!" he blurts out. "That was dumb."

Carol gives him a scornful look. "We're here, aren't we? If it was up to you, we'd never go anywhere."

Regan watches the surf crashing in, one wave after another. "But how are we going to get out again?"

Carol pulls off her soaked running shoes and tosses them in the dinghy. "We'll worry about that later. Now we're here, I'm for exploring the beach."

Regan hopes Matt will insist they leave, but Matt seems to have gotten over their near-calamity already.

He's off for a jog along the beach. Carol heads in the other direction, stopping every now and then to pick up a shell or examine a sculpted piece of driftwood.

Regan sighs, watching her go. *Talk to the wall.* After a while, he shrugs and decides he might as well enjoy it too. He stands in water up to his ankles, feeling the fine white sand run between his toes as the sea surges in and out, and stares down at the tiny fish darting around his feet. The sun, the cool salt water, the warm breeze make it so pleasant he would like to stay there forever. In the back of his mind, though, he's worrying about getting the dinghy out through that surf.

Carol's now at one end of the beach, Matt at the other. Regan shuffles along in the shallows, watching the tiny fish. Suddenly he hears a shout from Matt.

He looks up. Matt's racing back, pointing, and Regan turns to see that the stretch of beach is empty. The dinghy is floating away. Fast.

"Oh, no!" he exclaims. He sprints back, sees Matt race into the surf, spray flying. *Matt's going to catch up with it,* he thinks. *It's going to be okay.* Then he hears a yelp, sees Matt stop, limp back to the shore, and flop down in the sand in obvious pain.

Regan arrives, panting. Matt's holding his foot and grimacing. "Stepped on something," he says. "Don't know what, but it hurts like crazy."

Regan looks for blood. There isn't any, but he can see small black slivers embedded in the sole of Matt's foot, which is red and starting to swell. He imagines the foot swelling like a balloon, being cut off . . . Matt learning to walk all over again. . . .

Carol runs up and stares out at the dinghy. "What are you standing here for? We gotta go after it!"

Regan shakes his head. "Look what happened to Matt. It's dangerous out there."

"So he stepped on something," Carol says. "We can put on shoes."

"They're in the dinghy," Regan reminds her.

"I'm going after it anyway," Carol says, "even if you're too scared." She starts to wade in, but sees the dinghy is now a long way out and she hesitates.

"Here comes someone!" Regan shouts. Another dinghy is heading toward the runaway, a lone man driving.

"Someone in the harbor must've spotted it!" Matt says.

The driver motors over, grabs the bow line, and takes the dinghy in tow. He sees them and waves.

"But why's he stopping?" Carol asks. For the man has put his outboard in neutral and both dinghies are now drifting a hundred feet out from the beach. The man stands up, shouts something, which they can't hear, and gestures. Then he starts up again and they watch him tow their dinghy around a point of land to another, more protected stretch of beach.

They start walking, Matt with a pronounced limp.

"I couldn't land back there," the man explains, after they've thanked him and hauled their dinghy up on the new stretch of beach. "Never would have made it through that surf back there, towing a dinghy."

"We found out about the surf," Matt says. "Sure glad you saw our dinghy, sir."

"I'm anchored just over there," the man says, pointing. "Like to be by myself. I was watching the pelicans dive when I saw this empty dinghy. Knew something was wrong."

"Lucky for us," Regan says. He imagines losing the dinghy and having to tell their parents. *Don't even think about it,* he decides.

"You have to pull a dinghy way up on the beach here," the man says. "Otherwise the surf has a way of coming in and grabbing it. You kids okay now?"

They assure him they are, and the man says in that case he has an errand in town. They thank him again and help him push his dinghy out. As they wave good-bye, Regan sees another dinghy heading their way. The driver looks familiar.

"It's Anthony!" he shouts, as the other dinghy approaches. "I told you guys he was here!" He jumps up and down, waving excitedly.

"So it's Anthony," Matt says. "We gotta go."

Carol tries to launch their dinghy. "Yeah, c'mon, help me haul this out."

"Not till I see Anthony," Regan says stubbornly. He knows they can't leave without him and he doesn't intend to go until he's talked to his friend.

"I recognized your parents in town," Anthony says, when he's landed. "They said you were around the harbor somewhere, so I came looking."

They sit together on the side of Anthony's dinghy, while Regan tells him everything that happened at the other beach. Carol paces restlessly. When Regan comes to the part about Matt hurting his foot, Anthony asks to see it.

"You stepped on a sea urchin," he tells Matt. "They have these sharp black spines that come off and stay in your foot."

"It's paining something fierce," Matt says.

"I know, man, I did the same thing once. Only thing to do is pee on it – excuse me, Carol."

"What!" Matt says.

"Pee on it. Right now. The sooner the better."

Matt's eyes narrow. "You putting me on, Anthony?"

"No, honestly," Anthony assures him. "There's poison in those spines – that's why your foot's swelling. Urine has ammonia in it. Helps neutralize the poison."

Matt still looks doubtful. Anthony shrugs. "Up to you, but it'll ease the pain."

Matt gets up and limps toward a clump of bushes. "If you say so. Anything to stop this throbbing."

"I said ease it, not stop it," Anthony says. "It'll still throb for a while." He winks at Regan. "But only another week or so."

"Oh, great," Matt says, as he disappears behind a bush.

"Are you coming with us or not?" Carol says to Regan when Matt comes back. "'Cause we gotta go. We're late." This time Regan agrees. He helps push their dinghy out, after he and Anthony decide to meet up again in the morning.

"But you'll have to come early," Regan says. "We're leaving for Tobago Cays tomorrow morning."

"That's okay," Anthony tells him. "Grandpa starts work real early. We'll come by on the way to the boat he's working on."

"Wish you could come to Tobago Cays with us."

"Maybe we will," Anthony says. "After Grandpa finishes this job."

As they jump in the dinghy, Regan claims it's his turn to drive, but Carol tells him no way, he's lucky she even let him come. "We've had enough of your driving," Regan argues. "Look at all the trouble you got us into." He appeals to Matt, but Matt is suffering with his swollen foot and couldn't care less who drives so long as they don't bug him about it. Carol drives back.

At the dinghy dock their parents are waiting, looking anxious. The kids mumble apologies – they'd already agreed not to mention the near disaster in the surf, or the runaway dinghy. *About the only time the three of us have agreed on anything since we got here,* Regan muses.

Back on *Arcturus,* he wanders up on deck to his favorite place – the pulpit – a little seat formed by the V where the two side rails meet at the point of the bow. He sits watching the sky turn pink as the sun sinks. The pink deepens, turns to rose, and the sun seems about to fall into the sea. He almost expects to hear it sizzle. Then the sky darkens to purple and the first stars appear. It's all so sudden. Only seven o'clock and practically night already, which puzzles him at first because he's used to the long summer evenings at home. Then he remembers he's down south now, near the equator, where day and night are about equal all year around.

He watches the lights of an island freighter heading out to sea. For a moment he wishes he were on board. Going someplace where no one knows him, where he could start over again, become a different, braver person.

His mother's voice brings him back to reality, calling him to come and have some pizza while it's hot.

8

To and fro they were hurried about!
And to and fro, and in and out,

Early the next morning, Regan is in the cockpit munching on a piece of toast when he hears what he's been waiting for — a dinghy heading their way. The others are below, finishing breakfast.

It's Anthony driving, with a sturdy, gray-haired man in the bow. They pull alongside. "Hi, Regan," Anthony says. "This is my grandpa."

Regan's mother pokes her head out of the companionway. "Good morning. Come aboard and have a cup of coffee."

Soon everybody's in the cockpit and coffee cups are filled. Anthony's grandfather is talking sailing with Matt's father and mother, in between answering questions from Regan's mother about restaurants and Regan's father about bargain hunting.

"Think we can make Tobago Cays today, Mr. Waterman?" Matt's father asks.

"Call me Nate," Anthony's grandfather says. "You can make the Cays in a day, easy – it's downwind all the way. But you should start soon. You want to get there while there's good light – reefs and coral heads all over the place. Got a good chart?"

Matt's father spreads out the chart and everyone crowds around while Mr. Waterman traces the route from Bequia to the Cays. "Here's the safest way to approach," he tells them. "After you round Glossy Hill on Canouan – this island here – set a course of 230 degrees. Then, just before you reach Mayreau, head up into the wind and beat into the Cays, here." Regan peers over his shoulder to where his finger is. He sees four small green spots on the chart surrounded by x's.

"Be careful. This is all reef here," Mr. Waterman says, pointing to the string of x's. Regan doesn't like the look of all those x's. He notices something else too. There's nothing, other than the small island of Mayreau, to the east or to the west of the Cays. Nothing but blue water all the way to the edge of the chart.

Anthony's grandfather drains his cup and gets up. "Thanks for the coffee, folks. We've got to get moving – that engine repair job is waiting for me and my helper here. Maybe when we finish, we'll come on over to the Cays – all depends on whether I get any more rush calls. The Cays is a good place to get away – really isolated, specially now in the off-season. There won't be hardly any other boats there."

Great, Regan thinks, *Anthony may be coming. And no other boats — just us and them all by ourselves.* Then he has a second thought — *what if they don't make it and we're way off there alone?* He's not so sure he likes that idea.

Just as the dinghy is about to pull away, Mr. Waterman remembers something he heard on his VHF radio last night. A tropical storm out in the Atlantic is headed toward the Caribbean. "It could hit here in a day or two," he tells Matt's father. "On the other hand, it could miss us completely. Just keep an eye out. Not hurricane season yet, but it could be a good stiff blow."

Anthony takes one more look back at *Arcturus* as their dinghy accelerates away. He can see Regan and Matt making their way to the bow to haul up the anchor. "Looks like they're off already, Grandpa. Not wasting any time. Sure hope they don't get mixed up with any reefs over in the Cays."

"They'll be all right," his grandfather assures him. "I showed them the way to get in." He heads the dinghy toward the ketch *Starcatcher,* where they'll be working this morning. "We'll probably be there by tomorrow, if they need any help, but I doubt they will. Mr. O'Brien's done plenty of sailing before, so's Mrs. O'Brien."

Yes, but the others have a lot to learn, Anthony thinks, *specially about dinghies and surf and that sort of thing.* He wonders, too, how it will all work out for Regan with

Matt. They seemed to be getting along, he noticed –
well, sort of. He hopes Regan hangs in there.

As they board *Starcatcher,* the captain tells Mr.
Waterman there's been a call for him on the VHF radio
from the yacht *Fair Winds.* He passes over his handheld
VHF.

"Nate's Marine calling *Fair Winds*," Mr. Waterman
calls. A reply comes through and he strains to hear over
the static. "Wilco, over and out," he says, and signs off.
He makes another quick call, then thanks the captain and
goes below to get to work. Anthony follows to help
where he can – mostly handing his grandfather tools. He
doesn't mind being the gofer. He likes watching his
grandfather's skilled hands at work, and admires the way
he can make a balky engine purr, a dead bilge pump
come to life.

"These cruising folks going to keep us busy,
Anthony," his grandfather says, as he squeezes into the
cramped engine compartment. "I guess you heard *Fair
Winds* on the VHF just now. They're in a panic. Their
fridge quit on them and all their frozen food is spoiling."

"Are they anchored here too?" Anthony asks.

"No, they're over in Mustique – you know, where
the rich tourists go. Soon as we fix this engine here, we
gotta get over there and look after *Fair Winds.* And
there's another boat over there wants us too. They say
their batteries keep running down – can't keep up with
all their electrical gadgets." He shakes his head. "Too
many gadgets on these new boats, if you ask me. Should

go back to the old ways – ice boxes and coal oil lamps. KEEP IT SIMPLE ON A BOAT is my motto. Not so much to go wrong."

"Makes sense to me, Grandpa," Anthony says.

His grandfather laughs. "On the other hand, Anthony, it gives me a job fixing all that stuff for them." He takes another turn on the wrench he's using to adjust the diesel injectors. "But at this rate, we won't get to the Cays for a couple of days. I checked out the latest weather report while I was on the radio. That tropical storm is now just two hundred miles east and heading this way. They expect it'll hit here sometime tomorrow – we'd better warn your friends to get themselves well anchored until it blows over."

"Good idea, Grandpa," Anthony agrees.

But later, when his grandfather tries to reach *Arcturus*, there is no response. "Guess they don't have their VHF on," he says. "I'll try later."

He gets no response later either. "They're probably out of range by now. We'll get over to Tobago Cays soon as we can, but the storm may beat us to it."

Arcturus ghosts along under a cloudless sky in the light morning breeze. Aunt Shelley is behind the wheel; the others lounge in the cockpit, except for Regan. He stands by the winch, and when a wind shift comes along, he cranks in or lets out the sails as his aunt tells him. He's beginning to feel like a real sailor.

It's almost noon as they approach the island of

Canouan. Regan's mother scans the north end of the island through binoculars. "Looks like a pretty bay with a beach over there," she says. "And it's empty. Could we anchor there and have lunch?"

"We're making good time, why not?" Uncle Ron says. "I'll have a look at the chart." As he unrolls the chart, the others gather around to look. Regan sees there's only a few of those scary x's in the bay.

"But what's that yellow mean?" his mother asks. There's a band of yellow around the inside of the bay.

"Shallow water," Uncle Ron answers. "Be all right as long as we don't go too far in." He points to the x's scattered here and there. "And not too many reefs."

When they get to the bay, they drop the sails and Uncle Ron takes the wheel and starts the engine. At the far end, a small boat drifts with two fishermen in it. As *Arcturus* noses into the bay, the fishermen wave. "Friendly folk around here," Regan's mother says, waving back.

But the fishermen keep waving – more vigorously now, and shouting. "Maybe they're trying to tell us something," Matt's father says. Suddenly he tenses. "Oh, no!" He shoves the gear lever quickly into neutral, then into reverse. *Arcturus* slows but her forward momentum keeps her going.

Regan hears Matt draw in his breath. "What?" he asks. Matt points grimly to the depth gauge. Regan stares; they all stare. Most of the morning the gauge had been reading eighty or ninety feet. Now it read only ten feet!

"Damn!" Matt's father exclaims, for the gauge flashes nine feet now and an alarm light begins blinking. Regan remembers being told that *Arcturus* has a seven-foot keel. That means there's only two feet between their keel and the bottom.

Uncle Ron guns the engine in reverse. *Arcturus* has almost stopped, but not quite soon enough. Regan stares at the depth gauge, as if hypnotized. They all stare. Eight feet, seven point five. Suddenly . . . *clunk!* The sound comes from underneath his feet. *Clunk! . . . Clunk!* *Arcturus* grinds to a standstill. They're on the reef!

The engine roars. With a harsh scraping sound, *Arcturus* inches back, then shudders to a stop. A wave hits and shoves them ahead again. Regan winces as the keel scrapes noisily on coral. He runs below to see if water is pouring in — he's read that fiberglass hulls are only an inch or so thick, and coral is hard. There's no water, but he doesn't like being down there hearing the scraping sounds from underneath.

He dashes back up. His uncle is giving the engine full speed in reverse. *Arcturus* rocks, but doesn't move. "The dinghy!" his uncle yells, snatching a line from the locker. "The engine won't do it. We'll pull her off with the dinghy."

He takes Regan's father with him to help with the line, leaving Matt to pay it out as they pull away. When he comes to the end, Matt cleats the line and shouts, "Ready!"

Uncle Ron revs the outboard motor, while Aunt

Shelley guns *Arcturus*'s engine. Both propellors churn the water like giant eggbeaters. The tow line stretches tighter and tighter, until Regan is sure it will snap, fly back, and decapitate them all.

Arcturus doesn't budge.

By this time the fishermen have motored over. "We'll pull too," they offer, throwing them a line.

The two outboards roar. They skid about on the end of their tow lines like water bugs. *Arcturus* groans as the lines strain. Regan holds his breath. He feels her shift.

Then, suddenly, *Arcturus* floats free. Everyone cheers.

The fishermen come alongside. "Follow us," one of them says. "We'll guide you out of here." The other one's shaking his head. "Don't know how you got *this* far without hitting the reef, man."

"I didn't expect it. Guess I wasn't watching close enough," Uncle Ron admits. "But that chart isn't too accurate either. There's more reef here than it shows."

The fishermen nod. "You're right, man, those charts aren't near as good as local know-how."

Uncle Ron invites them aboard, but they say they have fish traps to attend to. He follows them out of the bay, zigging and zagging to avoid further patches of reef.

"We'll head straight for the Cays now," he says, once they're in the clear. "No more exploring strange bays for me."

Regan thinks that is an excellent idea.

2

O happy living things! no tongue
Their beauty might declare:

Matt's father throttles back, maneuvers carefully between several dark patches, and picks a spot to anchor behind one of the four cays that make up the Tobago Cays. "It'll be sheltered here," he says. Across the cay, on the windward side, the surf crashes endlessly. But here, tucked behind the cay and sheltered by it, only a gentle roll rocks *Arcturus*.

From a distance, Regan's first glimpse of Tobago Cays had been disappointing. *Just a bunch of tiny low-lying islands covered with scrubby-looking brush*, he thought. Then, as they sailed closer, he saw the sparkling colors that circled each cay like a necklace. Dark blue, where the water was deep, shading to light blue as it shallowed, then to turquoise, then light brown, then golden sand at the very edges. "How lovely," his mother exclaimed.

But here and there between the cays lurked ugly-looking dark patches. "Coral heads near the surface," Uncle Ron said, steering carefully past. "Could rip the bottom out of a boat. That's why no one sails at night around here."

Using Nathan Waterman's detailed directions, they negotiated the entrance to the Cays with surprisingly little difficulty. After their encounter with the reef earlier that day, Uncle Ron went dead slow and kept a close watch on the depth gauge.

Now, at a nod from his father, Matt lets go the anchor. "Let out lots of scope – there's plenty of room," his father tells him. "No other boats to worry about here." He shuts down the engine. As the diesel dies everyone stops what they're doing, struck by the sudden quiet. Not a sound except the muffled beat of surf in the distance. Not another boat in sight. . . .

"Let's snorkel!" Carol whoops, grabbing mask and flippers – *the best mask,* Regan notices, *the only one that fits properly.* She lets down the swim ladder on the stern and plunges in. Regan and Matt quickly follow and swim behind her to a small reef nearby. Struggling with his mask, Regan swallows a mouthful of salty water and has a coughing fit. He finally gets the mask adjusted and peers down.

Brilliantly colored fish of all sizes and shapes, just ten feet below him, are going about their business as if he isn't there. He feels like he's suddenly opened a window on another world. Schools of small electric blue fish flash by, followed by red ones with big eyes – squirrel fish, he knows from the guidebook. Sturdy green parrot fish nibbling at the coral send scraping noises resonating through the water. A sergeant major, a tiny yellow fish with black stripes, rushes at a much bigger fish that ventures too close to its coral home, driving off the intruder. Regan treads water, watching the tiny brave fish for a long time, admiring its courage.

They stay until a five-foot barracuda looms in the distance. It turns languidly and cruises their way. That sends them fleeing for the boat in a panic. Regan and Carol reach the ladder at the same moment. She pushes her way up ahead of him. "What the hell was that big silver thing?" she pants, stripping off her mask.

"A barracuda," Regan says, as he hurries up behind her. "Didn't you see the black spots on its side?"

"No, but I saw some big teeth."

Aunt Shelley is leafing through the Grenadines guidebook. "Late afternoon is the barracuda's feeding time," she reads.

"You mean, we could have been its supper!" Matt exclaims.

"It says here that Caribbean barracuda eat only other fish," she assures him. Still, no one ventures in again that day – they decide they'll do their snorkeling in the mornings. Uncle Ron, however, dons mask and flippers and dives down to check the bottom of *Arcturus*.

"Just a bit of paint scraped off," he announces, as he

climbs back in. "Lucky those fishermen pulled us off before there was any real damage."

The next morning the weather is perfect. A cloudless sky, a steady breeze from the east – the same as the day before. *Every day must be like this down here,* Regan thinks. *No wonder Anthony misses it so much.*

After breakfast, Regan's mother suggests visiting each of the cays. They crowd into the dinghy, and Regan and Carol have a tussle over who's going to run the outboard until their father orders Regan to sit down.

On one of the cays they find a group of fishermen repairing their nets, and Aunt Shelley buys red snappers from them for dinner. Regan notices a vast reef spreading along the leeward side of this cay.

"Let's snorkel, Matt," he says quietly, so his sister won't hear.

His mother has other ideas. "Not now, Regan. It's time to head back for lunch."

"Aw, Mom."

"Maybe this afternoon," she adds, relenting. "But one of us will have to come with you."

After lunch, however, when Regan tries to get someone to come with them, Uncle Ron is busy putting up an awning, his mother has had enough sun for one day, his father too, and Aunt Shelley is having a nap in the hammock strung on deck.

"They'll be all right on their own," Uncle Ron says, examining the sky. It's all blue except for a few drifting clouds, puffy white ones like balls of cotton. "They won't be far away. Just on the other side of that cay."

Regan's mother agrees reluctantly. "Well, I suppose so – they're good swimmers. But only if Carol goes with them."

Regan jumps quickly into the dinghy to stake his claim as driver. "If the weather changes, you come right back," his mother warns.

He has to crank the outboard three times before it starts. And when it does, it sputters and almost dies before finally roaring to life. "Funny," he mutters. "It started first pull before."

"You just don't have the knack," Carol taunts. Regan has a feeling it's more than that. But if he suggests there's something wrong with the outboard, that will be the end of their snorkeling expedition. *When we come back, I'll tell Uncle Ron,* he promises himself. He revs the motor. It sputters once, twice, like it's in pain, then smooths out.

At the last minute, his mother makes them wait while she goes below and gathers up jackets, towels, and a plastic jug of water. She hands them down. "You'll be cold and thirsty when you come out."

It takes only a few minutes to circle the cay to the other side. The fishermen have left and they have the big reef to themselves. Regan cuts the motor between the reef and the cay and Matt throws out the small dinghy anchor.

Regan is still fiddling with his mask as Matt and

Carol jump in. "Come on, slowpoke," Carol urges. Then she and Matt strike out for the reef without him.

Regan is about to follow when he notices the dark cloud. He pushes up his mask and stares. It seems to have come out of nowhere. Still far away on the eastern horizon, it's a nasty, greeny black color and so low it seems to be touching the water.

Should he call the others back, insist they leave? Carol will call him a worrywart, and Matt will be more convinced than ever that he's a wimp. He shrugs. *Even if it's coming this way, it'll be a long time before it gets here. I'll keep an eye on it.* He pulls down his mask and jumps in.

Before he even reaches the reef, he sees a spotted ray gliding over the sand, and a sea turtle munching grass. Little squid follow him, curious, staring fixedly at him, and a swarm of blue tangs slide by in formation, like a flock of birds. He forgets the time and the weather, entranced by the parade of life down there. Until a shadow suddenly dims his underwater world.

Regan looks up quickly and knows right away it's time to leave. Past time. The same greeny black cloud is rolling straight toward them; he can't believe how fast it got there. And behind it, the rest of the sky is dark – all the way to the horizon. Gusts of wind are whipping up waves. He suddenly remembers Anthony's grandfather saying a tropical storm was coming.

He shouts at Carol, but she has her mask in the water and doesn't hear him. He swims over, taps her on the shoulder, and points to the sky.

When she sees the cloud, Carol doesn't hesitate. She calls Matt and the three of them strike out for the dinghy. There's no arguing about running the outboard this time — instinctively they all recognize that the strange eerie color of the sky spells danger.

Carol gets the outboard ready to go, while Matt and Regan haul up the dinghy anchor. She yanks the starter cord. Nothing happens. She yanks again. Not even a cough. She pumps the gas bulb and yanks again. Still nothing.

"Let me try," Matt says. They change places. He fiddles with the controls and pulls. Nothing. Again and again he pulls. The motor doesn't even sputter.

Regan looks around wildly. The wind is blowing them away from the cay. Fast. He scrambles to get out the oars.

10

And now the Storm-blast came and he
Was tyrannous and strong;
He struck with his o'ertaking wings,
And chased us south along.

While Matt struggles with the outboard, Regan battles to row them back to the cay. But no matter how hard he tries, he can't make any headway against the wind. And the mounting waves hammer at the bow of the dinghy as if they, too, are determined to hold it back.

He has to stop to catch his breath. A fierce gust sends the lightweight dinghy skittering even farther away. "Keep rowing!" Carol yells at him. She's crouched in the bow, hanging on, bouncing with each wave.

Regan turns and sees with dismay that the cay, and the mast of *Arcturus* sticking up behind it, are getting smaller by the minute. "Take . . . one . . . oar . . . Carol," he puffs, and she drops into the seat beside him.

They row until their arms ache, but each time they pause for breath the wind takes over and they lose more than they gained.

Matt's still bent over the outboard. He unscrews the top of the gas tank and peers in. "Lots of gas. Must be sand or something in the needle valve."

"Can you fix it?" Regan asks. He's afraid he knows the answer.

Matt shakes his head. "No tools." He looks up and, for the first time, sees how far out they've been blown. His eyes grow large. "Wow!" He grabs Regan's oar and paddles furiously. "We gotta get back there!"

But the wind is stronger now. It takes control and drives the dinghy across the water. Regan stumbles to the stern, yanks on the starter. Nothing. If only they had tried to start the motor *before* they'd pulled up the anchor. They would still have been close enough to get to the beach somehow. But they didn't. *One mistake like that and we're in big trouble,* he thinks. *There's nothing but open sea where the wind is taking us. We're done for, unless —*

"Hey, they're coming for us!" Carol yells suddenly.

Regan stares at the mast of *Arcturus* behind the cay. *She's right — it's moving!*

Carol stands up, waves both arms, her blond hair streaming out behind her. "Here!" she screams, staggering as a wave rocks the dinghy. "Out here!" But the wind takes her voice and throws it back.

No way they'll hear us this far away, Regan knows. *They won't even spot the dinghy until they round the end of the cay.* He stares hard, willing the mast to move faster. Then he sees something else.

Beyond the cay, beyond the mast, a solid curtain of rain is sweeping across the water. The rain comes on fast, reaches the cay, and suddenly he can't see anything – not the cay, not the mast of *Arcturus,* not anything but the gray curtain of rain.

They struggle into their jackets as the downpour reaches them. It hits with a blast of wind that rocks the dinghy. "Sit on the bottom!" Matt yells, and they slide down, huddle together on the floorboards, and hang on.

Regan ducks as a wave sends spray flying at them. The rain buckets down. He never would have believed it could rain like that. He can't see more than a few feet in any direction. It's raining so hard, it flattens the waves. So hard, it fills the dinghy until the water is sloshing over the floorboards.

Matt grabs the bailer from under the seat – a plastic jug cut in half – and begins scooping out water.

The rain goes on and on; they bail and bail, taking turns now. Regan wonders briefly if they should save some of the rainwater for later, but they have the whole jug of water his mother made them bring. Surely that will be enough till they're found.

Carol keeps staring into the downpour, as if she expects to see *Arcturus* appear any minute. "We should make a racket so they can find us," she shouts over the drumming of the rain.

Huddled in his jacket, Matt shrugs. "They won't be going anywhere in this. They probably think we're sheltering on the cay. As soon as the rain eases up and they can see where they're going, they'll come looking for us."

But the rain doesn't ease up. Not for hours. And by then, it's growing dark.

Regan watches the light fade with a feeling of dread. He knows what that means and he knows Matt and Carol do too. But none of them say it – it's too scary to even talk about. For the fading light means their parents can't come for them now. *Arcturus* would never make it with all those reefs surrounding the anchorage. Not until dawn.

Which means, they'll be out here all night.

Regan shudders as that realization hits home. He stares into the void, hoping against hope for a glimpse of a light. But there isn't any light – isn't anything to be seen in any direction. Nothing but the flash of whitecaps as the waves roll endlessly past.

The rain eases finally and then stops, and the wild gusts of wind calm down. A few stars come out as the sky begins to clear. The waves, however, mount in size, the aftermath of the storm. Huge, some of them. Huge swells that could flip their dinghy over like a leaf in the wind.

Regan knows from looking at the charts on the boat that there are no islands out here. Nothing to break those swells, to give them shelter. He tries not to think of the night ahead. Are Matt and Carol as scared as he is? Matt *sounds* calm. "Watch out – big one coming!" Matt warns now. He's still at the oars, fighting to keep the dinghy running straight on the backs of the swells that come up from behind.

In the stern, Regan hangs on as a swell picks up the dinghy and shoves it along. It's not the storm anymore, it's the swells that are the danger now. And they, like the wind, are pushing them farther and farther west — away from the cays, away from help, away from any hope of being found in a hurry.

11

The ship drove fast, loud roared the blast,
And southward aye we fled.

Matt's been at the oars so long he has blisters on his palms. "We'll take over, Matt," Carol says. Teetering in the rocking dinghy, she and Regan cautiously change places with Matt. They each take an oar.

"All you can do is try to ride out the swells," Matt says. "Don't let the dinghy get sideways to them, whatever you do. If a big one hits us sideways, we're goners."

As if it heard him, the biggest swell yet comes out of the night. Sweeping up from behind, it lifts the dinghy and pushes it forward with a rush. As they pick up speed, the bow begins to swing toward Regan's side.

"Pull, Regan!" Carol yells. "Harder!"

It's all up to him now, he knows. He rows furiously. Slowly the bow swings back. The dinghy careens down the face of the wave, faster and faster. Then, just as it appears they will lose control, the wave passes under them with a sighing sound and they slide down its back. The dinghy slows again.

Regan slumps over his oar. He waits, dreading the moment the next big one pounces on them from behind. Matt, a shape in the stern, bails the water that slopped in when the last wave broke. They've been at this for hours. They're too tired to talk.

A smaller swell lifts the dinghy, then passes underneath. Regan is trying to keep count. It seems to him that every seventh or eighth one is bigger than the others. Those are the dangerous ones.

He loses all track of time. He's lying against the side when he hears a rumbling sound. Jerking upright, he stares into the darkness behind them. Then he sees it approaching out of the night, its white top glistening. "Carol!" he howls.

She looks up and shrieks. A wall of water is thundering down on them.

The wave towers above them, its top curling. Twice as high as anything they've faced yet. Like a building toppling over on them.

"Hang on!" Matt yells.

For a moment, time stands still. Paralyzed, they stare up at it. Then the forward edge reaches them and the dinghy is picked up and thrown ahead. As if by a giant's hand.

"Row!" Carol shouts. "Keep it straight!" Regan sits in a trance of fear, his hand frozen on the oar. The dinghy is surfing now, tearing along on the front of the monstrous wave, which hisses and rumbles behind them. Its foamy top slams into the stern, half-filling the dinghy. It grabs Regan's oar and rips it out of his hands. He makes a lunge for it. Too late. The oar disappears over the side.

Out of control now, the wave in charge, the dinghy tilts sharply, hovers in the air. Regan throws himself to the high side. He glimpses Carol struggling to hold on, hears a shout from Matt in the stern. The dinghy hangs momentarily at a crazy angle. *We're going over!* Regan thinks. *We're finished!* He feels himself slipping, claws at the rubber fabric, but there's nothing to grip. He braces for the shock of the wave closing over him, sweeping him away. Then he's in the sea.

The wave tumbles him wildly, like laundry in a washing machine. He struggles to the surface, takes a gasp of air, then he's shoved under again. The life he'll never live flashes before him – he'll never become an Olympic swimmer, win a medal, make his father proud, go to college, be a scientist. . . .

Something hard and rubbery whacks him on the head. The dinghy. He reaches up and tries to grab it, but his hand slips off and he goes under again. He feels a pressure on his arm. Something's got hold of him, something's dragging him along. The next thing he knows, he's hauled upwards and plopped unceremoniously on the floorboards. He coughs up water. Carol's standing over him, still hanging on to his arm.

He lifts his head, looks around. Miraculously, the

dinghy has settled back on an even keel. The towering crest has passed and they're sliding down the back of the wave. Already it's rumbling off into the night.

It takes a moment for him to realize what happened. The weight of water in the half-filled dinghy must have saved them. That weight kept the dinghy from flipping over and slowed it down enough for the monster to roll by underneath.

Carol is the first to speak. "God, I thought you were done for. I thought we were all done for."

"I would have been if you hadn't grabbed me," Regan says. He has no doubt about that.

Matt picks up the bailer. "I've heard of rogue waves before, but I never thought they could be *that* big!"

So that's what it was, Regan realizes with a shock. *A rogue wave. We were hit by a rogue wave and survived.*

"If we can make it through that, we can make it through anything," Carol says.

"Maybe," Regan puts in. "But we've only got one oar now. I lost mine."

He waits for Carol to chew him out. Losing that oar, he knows, has ruined any chance of them going anywhere under their own steam.

"You couldn't help it, Regan," she says. "I nearly lost mine, too."

He stares up at her in surprise. Is this his big sister, Carol? His tormentor?

The sea is calmer now, as if the rogue wave has flattened everything in its path like a steamroller. The dinghy rides the tamer swells more easily. Soon Regan stops worrying about the next big one. He leans against the side and closes his eyes. He can feel the dinghy going up and down, up and down, up and down. . . .

12

Day after day, day after day,
We stuck, nor breath nor motion;
As idle as a painted ship
Upon a painted ocean.

He's in the water, trying to get away. Something big is chasing him. He flails his arms and legs uselessly – he's forgotten how to swim! It's gaining on him. He sees a gaping jaw, a row of jagged teeth. He tries to scream. . . .

Regan sits up with a start, opens his eyes. His racing heartbeat calms. A nightmare, that's all. Then he remembers where he is. He shivers. That's a nightmare too. The whole terrible night. But a nightmare that hasn't gone away even though he's awake now. They're still out there, still in the dinghy. Still adrift. Still lost at sea.

He glances at the sky. *It's changed*, he realizes suddenly – *not as pitch-dark now*. He stares. Yes, there it is, a pale fringe of light on the horizon. *Dawn!* They've made it through the night. Through the storm, through the rogue wave, through all the terrors that threatened them. *Dawn*. They made it. He feels like cheering.

The predawn wind is light, the swells long and rolling now – nothing like the monstrous ones in the night. He scans the horizon, sure that he'll see an island, a boat, a sail – something.

But there's nothing. Nothing as far as the eye can see. Nothing but water, stretching to the horizon in every direction. No matter which way he turns, it's the same empty sea.

So much emptiness. He never imagined there could be so much emptiness in the whole world. He doesn't feel like cheering now.

But they'll come for us, he tells himself. *Now that it's light, they'll come for us. Arcturus will come sailing over the horizon anytime now.* First he'll see her white sails, then her golden yellow hull, then the whole boat, with Uncle Ron at the wheel and his mother and father and aunt straining their eyes, waving frantically. Then they'll be alongside, helping them aboard and taking them below for scrambled eggs and toast. Everyone will be laughing and crying and hugging them. Even his father will hug him.

And then he remembers the book he read back in Toronto – the sailor who'd drifted for months because his tiny life raft was so hard to spot in a huge ocean. As hard to spot as a tiny dinghy. *Only this isn't the Atlantic Ocean,* he tells himself, *it's only the Caribbean.*

But wait! What was it Anthony told him? That the

Caribbean Sea was a thousand miles across and mostly empty. A thousand miles of empty sea. And Anthony knows the Caribbean.

Carol opens her eyes and frowns. She looks at him with a puzzled expression, as if wondering what he's doing in her cabin. Suddenly, as it all comes back to her, she sits up and stares out at the water. Then she scrambles to her feet, braces herself, and searches the horizon.

"Not one boat. Why aren't they out looking for us?"

Matt's awake now and he has a good look around too. "I'm sure they are."

"Well, where are they then?" Carol demands, as if it's his fault.

Matt shrugs. "They couldn't leave the Cays till first light. But they'll be searching now. Lots of boats will be searching, maybe even the U.S. Coast Guard."

"Give them time," Regan adds. "It's like looking for a needle in a haystack."

Carol snorts. "We can't have drifted that far. Needle in a haystack – huh!"

That's my sister, her old feisty self again, Regan thinks. *Can't tell her anything.* But he suspects she's wrong. He trails his hand over the side and watches the water ripple past his fingers. "See those ripples?" he says. "That means we're moving, drifting farther away all the time. And who knows how far the storm blew us last night?"

Carol squints at him. "So what are you trying to say – that they won't find us?"

"No, I'm just saying it might take them a while."

"We ought to be able to guess how far we've drifted," Matt says. He knits his brow and Regan can see his lips moving. Matt might be the best athlete in their class, but he isn't the brightest in math.

Carol picks up the water jug and takes a swig. "Anyway, I'm sure glad Mom made us bring this water."

"Yeah, and our jackets too," Regan says. He thinks of all the times he's complained about his mother fussing over him. He takes a swig from the jug. When it hits his empty stomach, he realizes how hungry he is.

A small flying fish breaks the surface, skims the waves for twenty feet, then slices back in.

"I'm so hungry I could eat one of those raw," he says. "Like Steven Callahan."

"Steven who?" asks Carol.

"Callahan. He was a shipwrecked sailor I read about. He drifted in his life raft for . . . for a long time. He caught fish and ate them raw to stay alive."

Carol makes a face. "Yuck – no thanks. I'll wait. Shouldn't be long now." She lays back against the side.

"I'm not so sure about that," Matt says, scratching his head. He's still trying to work out how far they've drifted. "The way that wind was blowing last night, I figure it must have pushed us along at two miles an hour at least. And the current here runs at two miles an hour – I saw that on Dad's chart. So that's four miles an hour. That means –"

"Anthony told me the wind always blows from east

to west," Regan interrupts. "But which way does the current go?"

"The same way, more or less. East to west. Now where was I? . . ." Matt wrinkles his brow.

Regan helps him out. "Four miles an hour for twelve hours, that's . . ." He blanches. "That's forty-eight miles!"

"Forty-eight miles!" Carol sits up abruptly.

13

All in a hot and copper sky,
The bloody Sun, at noon,
Right up above the mast did stand,
No bigger than the Moon.

"Forty-eight miles!" Carol glares at Regan. "You're crazy. We couldn't have been blown *that* far."

"'Fraid he's right, Carol," Matt says. "Forty-eight miles and getting farther away all the time."

At that, Carol stands up and stares at the horizon, her hands on her hips, her mouth set. She stays that way a long time. When she sits down again, she appears to have made up her mind about something.

"All right," she declares finally. "All right, maybe we *have* gone forty-eight miles; maybe they *will* take a while to find us. So we'd better not just sit here like dummies. We'd better do something about it."

"Do?" Regan says. "What can we *do?* The motor's dead and we're down to one oar."

"We can get ready," his sister says firmly.

"Get ready for what?" Matt and Regan chorus.

"To survive, that's what." She scowls at them. "'Cause I don't know about you guys, but I'm going to survive till they get here."

Suddenly, unbelievably, Regan feels like hugging her. Carol, his tormentor for as long as he can remember. Her confidence, her cockiness, her combativeness – the very things that bug him at home – are exactly what they need out here. He stares at her for the first time with admiration.

"First thing is the water," she announces. "From now on, we ration the water."

Regan and Matt both nod in agreement.

She holds up the water jug, already half-empty. "So how long does this have to last us?"

Silence.

She looks at Regan. "How long did this Steven Callahan guy drift before he was rescued?"

Regan gazes out at the sea. "Uh, I forget exactly."

"Don't give me that. You remember everything you read."

All right, Regan thinks, *she asked for it.* "Seventy-six days," he says.

She stares at him. "But they weren't really looking for him, right?"

"They were looking. But it's awful hard to find a little raft in a big ocean."

"Well, he must have been unlucky," Carol says flatly. She eyes the water jug again. "Tell you what – we each get two drinks a day. By the time the water's gone, we'll be rescued. Or it'll rain, one or the other."

She tucks the jug under the seat. "Now for food. Did that guy really eat raw fish?"

"That was all he had," Regan says. "It was that or starve."

"How'd he catch them?"

"He had a speargun in his emergency kit."

Carol makes a face. "That's a lot of help."

"There's other ways to catch fish," Regan counters. He reaches down, picks up the end of the bow line. "Maybe we can rig up something with this."

Carol looks at him for a minute, as if she were seeing a different Regan too. More than just a pest of a brother. "Yeah, maybe we can," she agrees. A thought strikes her and she digs in her jacket pocket. "Hey, I've got a safety pin! We could use it for a hook." She holds the pin up triumphantly.

"And I've got my sailor's knife to cut some line," Matt says.

"So there we are," Regan says. But when he tries to imagine eating raw fish, he almost gags. He's hungry, really hungry, but not that hungry. The others don't seem to be ready to eat raw fish yet either. Carol puts her pin away. "Maybe later," she says. "If they still haven't found us."

The sun is up now. As it climbs the eastern sky, it blazes down on the dinghy without mercy. They soak their towels in seawater and put them over their heads.

The water cools them, but it leaves their skin salty and itchy.

Slowly, the morning wears on. Regan's mouth is so dry, he can hardly swallow. He dunks his towel again and lets the water run over his head and down his back. It's tempting to drink some, but he doesn't dare – he still remembers a scene from an old movie about a steamer sunk by a submarine during the war. One of the survivors, adrift in a lifeboat, gave in to temptation and drank seawater. He went mad.

The three sprawl on the floorboards, half asleep, hot, thirsty, hungry, and cranky. They've taken out the plastic seat and thrown it overboard to make room to stretch out, but Regan finds he can't move without bumping Carol or Matt and getting a dirty look. He lies there and tries not to think how far down the ocean goes beneath them. *Half a mile, maybe? And what's down there, circling, waiting for us? All that's keeping us up is this rubber dinghy full of air.*

Stop thinking about it, he tells himself, *think about something else, think about school, think about –*

Thump! Something whacks him on the rear. He glares at Matt, then at Carol, but they're both sprawled motionless.

Another blow. He jumps up.

Mat leans out over the rubber gunwale. "Hold my legs," he tells Carol. He peers under the dinghy, his hair in the water. "I see a tail!" he calls back. "A big yellow tail."

Regan leans over the other side. A large fish, about three feet long with a blunt head, swims into view. As he watches, it turns, glides back underneath, and thumps the bottom again. He remembers then something he read in the sailor's story. "It's after the barnacles!"

Carol gives him a puzzled look. "The barnacles?"

"Yeah, that must be it," Matt says. "Barnacles grow on the bottom of boats. It's knocking them off and eating them. We gotta stop it!"

Carol stamps on the floorboards. "Go away, you!"

Thump! Thump!

"It'll punch a hole in the bottom!" Matt howls. But just then a small flying fish breaks the surface nearby and the big yellow-tailed fish shoots out from under the dinghy after it, moving so fast it's only a blur. Suddenly it's gone.

They slump back with sighs of relief. Silence settles over the dinghy again.

Regan stares at the water bottle. "Must be time for a drink," he croaks.

Carol shakes her head stubbornly. "Wait a little longer." Her voice has gone croaky too.

She's right, Regan knows. *We have to wait.* "Set a time then," he says hoarsely. Maybe it'll be easier to wait if he knows when it's coming.

"How can I?" Carol snaps. "No watch."

"At noon," he persists. "We'll have a drink at noon."

Carol shrugs. "Suits me. But how do we know when it's noon?"

Regan points straight up. "When the sun gets there. At the zenith."

It seems to take forever. The sun's climb is tortuously slow. Regan wants to swallow, but he has no saliva left. His throat feels as dry and scratchy as a lizard's skin. The time drags by. He can't take his eyes off the water jug.

They wait and wait, then wait some more, until at last the sun is directly overhead. Carol picks up the jug and passes it to Regan. "One mouthful each, that's all we can spare. No cheating."

He lifts the jug to his lips with shaky hands and takes a mouthful. Only water, but so sweet, so delicious. He holds the water in his mouth as long as he can, savoring it before he lets it trickle down his parched throat. It isn't enough. Not nearly enough. Instantly, his mouth is dry again and crying out for more. He passes the jug to Matt, who takes his turn and silently passes it to Carol. Carol takes her mouthful, then wraps the precious jug in her jacket to keep it cool.

It isn't long after his drink that Regan gets the urge. "Turn the other way," he says to Carol. "I have to pee."

He stands in the stern beside the motor. Balancing with the waves, he stares down at his yellow stream. Then, something makes him look up and he sees it. In the distance, on the horizon, a small dark shape.

14

Water, water, everywhere,
And all the boards did shrink;
Water, water, everywhere,
Nor any drop to drink.

"Hey, look!" Regan cries. It's a long way off, but he can make out a funnel and a brown hull.

"It's a freighter!" Matt yells.

Carol leaps up, cheering. "We're saved!"

They stand, waiting breathlessly for it to come closer. Regan imagines the throbbing of the engine, the freighter growing bigger and bigger, the crew on deck staring at them in astonishment. But it doesn't get bigger – it stays the same size, like a toy ship inching across the horizon.

"We have to signal it!" Carol says. "Make them see us." She grabs a yellow and orange striped towel and waves it over her head. "Come on, freighter!" she screams. "Look this way!"

They wave and shout until they're hoarse. Still the

freighter keeps moving relentlessly across the horizon. *Like those ducks in a shooting gallery,* Regan thinks. *Going by but never coming any closer.*

Their shouts get feebler and feebler; the ship, smaller and smaller. Then it slides from view and they collapse back onto the floorboards.

No one says anything for a long time. *To get up your hopes, to see a ship and watch it disappear again,* Regan decides, *is worse than not seeing one at all.*

The sun is burning hot now and there's no shelter from it, except their towels. Regan knows Carol is suffering the most because of her fair skin. She's always been a fast burn. Her nose and her shoulders are beet red, but she doesn't complain. *You have to give her that,* he thinks, *she's not a complainer.* As the blazing sun slowly makes its way across the sky, they doze fitfully.

Regan wakes up with a cooling breeze on his cheek. The sun is sinking at last. He sits up, stretches, and looks around. That's when he sees the gray triangle. It's gliding soundlessly toward them, heading straight for the dinghy.

He can tell it isn't a dolphin this time. The fin doesn't move up and down like a dolphin's fin. It slices through the water as steady as the periscope of a submarine. He tries to cry out a warning to the others. The cry sticks in his throat. All he can do is poke them and point. As the shark closes in, its streamlined body, as long as the dinghy, and its wicked-looking snout show clearly below the surface.

It circles twice then dives underneath, nudging the dinghy from below.

Regan hardly dares breathe. "What's it going to do?" he whispers hoarsely to Matt.

Matt's eyes are big. "How do I know?" he whispers back.

The shark makes another leisurely circle of the dinghy. Regan feels as if it's examining them . . . seeing if they're worth the bother . . . figuring out how to get at them. He imagines the rows of sharp teeth and shivers.

The shark circles and slides underneath again. The dinghy rocks as the shark brushes against the bottom.

Carol snatches up the remaining oar. She stands with it poised, like a harpoon. "Leave us alone!" she shouts.

"Don't make it mad!" Matt cries out. "Stop her, Regan!"

But Regan remembers what Anthony told him about sharks. They don't take chances – they don't have to, they're masters of their domain. They avoid any encounter that might injure them and change them from hunter to prey. And they have one particularly sensitive spot.

"Aim at its nose," he whispers. "The tip."

Carol stares at him. Again that look, as if she's seeing him for the first time.

The shark circles closer, brushing the side of the dinghy with a harsh scraping sound, like sandpaper. Carol strikes. She scores a hit. The oar jabs the shark's snout and instantly, with a flick of its long body, it dives out of sight.

They hold their breath and wait. Regan pictures the shark in the depths – *will it wander off to hunt elsewhere? Or will it turn angrily, get up speed to take a run at our flimsy dinghy?*

No one moves. Time passes.

"I think you scared it off!" he says finally. "Good going, Carol. You hit it just right." He was amazed at her cool nerve.

She shrugs. "I wasn't going to let a stupid shark sink us. But it was you who told me where to aim."

Matt sighs with relief. "I sure hope we never see *him* again."

But Regan doubts they've seen the last of the shark. *Maybe for today, but what about tomorrow at feeding time?*

Matt is busy studying the sky. Masses of clouds are building up in the east. "Thunderheads," he says. "If they blow this way, we might get rain tonight." He seems to have forgotten about the shark already. *Lucky guy, he gets over things easily,* Regan thinks.

He watches as the clouds pile higher. Great tall thunderheads, like giant cauliflowers. He tries to imagine taking a big drink of rainwater, all he wants. *Bliss.*

"We need something to catch the rain in," Matt says.

"We could use one of the jackets," Regan suggests. "You know, stretch it out between the three of us like a fireman's net." They try it. The nylon jacket, it seems, will do the job – if they *do* get rain.

A bolt of lightning shoots through the clouds. It takes a minute for the thunder to reach them – a long rolling rumble, like a warning. Those clouds, Regan realizes, could be their salvation, bringing them water, but those clouds could also bring another storm. A trial they would have to go through to get the treasure that comes with it. He remembers the storm that battered them the night before and shudders.

In the west, the sky is still cloudless, the sun just beginning to set. The blazing color contrasts with the massive thunderheads in the east. Regan sits watching, swiveling his head from the one dramatic scene to the other. It reminds him of sitting in church beside his parents when he was very small, listening to the thunder of the organ and watching the multi-colored light streaming through the stained-glass windows. But that was nothing like this.

As darkness closes in, they watch and wait for rain. But now the thunderheads seem to be moving as much north as east. They may pass to the north of them.

"Maybe we'll still get the edge of it," Matt says, hopefully. They have the jacket ready to catch the rain the minute it starts. They don't want to miss a drop. Regan licks his parched lips and tries to swallow as he follows the jagged slashes of lightning. It's much cooler and the wind has picked up. Now and then a wave breaks and water splashes in.

They wait until far into the night, but in the end the storm passes by to the north. Regan can hardly bear the thought of all that precious water being dumped somewhere else. He sighs and puts on his jacket.

They huddle together on the floorboards for warmth and the comfort of each other's presence. *Funny,* he thinks, *a few days ago I never would have wanted, or dared, to be this close to Carol.* He tries to forget his thirst, his hunger, his fear. And finally he sleeps.

15

The Sun came up upon the left,
Out of the sea came he!
And he shone bright, and on the right
Went down into the sea.

Regan wakes as the sky is beginning to lighten in the east. He's sandwiched between Matt and Carol and has to lever himself up so as not to disturb them. Carol mutters once, then goes back to sleep. Matt doesn't stir.

The darkness lifts gradually, like a curtain going up on some gigantic stage. Methodically he scans the horizon, a habit now – the whole circle, 360 degrees. All he sees is the same empty sea.

The horizon at sea, he remembers reading somewhere, is five miles away. That means they are the only living things in a circle ten miles across. Other than the fish, of course. And the sharks. And the occasional flock of storm petrels – the plucky little birds that live their lives at sea – skimming the waves.

His stomach gurgles and he realizes how hungry he

is. He's never known real hunger before. He can't help thinking about burgers and fries, followed by a big slice of lemon meringue pie. But right now he'd eat anything, even the things he hates most, like brussels sprouts. He can imagine eating a whole plateful of brussels sprouts. Just wolfing them down.

He holds up the jug to check the water level. Not much left. Carol stirs and he quickly tucks the jug away in case she wakes up and thinks he's cheating on them. But he's seen enough to know they'll run out today. They have ten days after that. Humans can live ten days without water, it said in the sailor's book. That was for grown-ups with flesh on their bones, not skinny kids like him. Carol would last longer than him, so would Matt. He decides not to think about that anymore.

Clumps of seaweed drift alongside. He spots a piece of driftwood tangled in one of the clumps and remembers standing beside the Don River with Matt, back in Toronto. Seems so long ago. Could this be the piece of driftwood he threw into the Don? Not likely . . . and yet . . .

A sudden splash beside the dinghy. Regan jumps. *What now?*

Another splash and the flick of something silver. He leans out, shades his eyes and peers under the dinghy. A small fish, not even a foot long, peers back at him. He sees another, and another, and another. A whole school of the little silvery fish is gathered there.

He picks up the only line they have, the bow line, and examines it. It's made of many separate strands. He begins to unravel one.

"What's up?" Matt's awake and watching him.

"Fish. Under the dinghy – little fish. Maybe we can catch one."

Matt sits up, interested. "Yeah, let's try."

Carol sits up too and watches.

Matt takes out his knife and cuts the strand. Carol digs out her pin. It's a big safety pin, shiny and sturdy. Regan opens it, spreads the two arms apart, then ties the line around the pinhead. He dangles it over the side and watches.

The pin revolves slowly a few feet below the surface. A fish swims up and stares at it, then backs away. Others gather around. One even nibbles at the pin, but doesn't take it in its mouth. After a while the fish seem to lose interest.

"Need bait," Matt says.

"Guess so," Regan agrees. If only he can catch one, he'll have bait to catch more. But he's been up only a short while and he's exhausted already. Without food or water, he doesn't have any energy left. All he wants to do is lie down, and all he can think about is eating and drinking. He wraps the line around the oar, leaving the pin dangling in the water just in case. Maybe one of the fish will mistake it for a shiny worm or something. He stretches out to rest with the oar under his arm.

The morning seems exactly the same as the morning before. A light wind from the east, which will likely build as the day goes on, rolling swells that lift the dinghy in a regular rhythm. But something is different today. He puzzles over that until he suddenly realizes what it is.

The dinghy is riding lower in the water!

Alarmed, he sits up and presses his index finger into the side, testing it. His finger sinks in easily. He frowns. When they started out, the sides had been as taut as a drum. Now they were soft, like a . . . like what? Like a bicycle tire that's been punctured!

"Hey, Matt!" he cries, as the terrible truth dawns. "We've sprung a leak!"

Strangely, Matt doesn't react.

But Carol sits up abruptly. "We've what!"

"Sprung a leak," he says to her. "Watch!" He presses the side again.

They both look at Matt, the expert.

He shrugs. "All inflatable dinghies lose air. Little by little. Some are worse than others. Nothing we can do about it – the air pump's back on *Arcturus*."

He already knew, Regan thinks. *He already knew but he wasn't going to tell us.* "But feel how soft it is!" he insists.

"I know," Matt says. "Back home I have to pump up our dinghy every week."

"But . . . but . . . we'll sink!" Regan splutters.

Matt doesn't say anything.

"Won't we?" he persists.

"Not for a while," Matt says.

"And we'll be rescued before then," Carol puts in quickly. Too quickly.

Suddenly the oar with the line around it rattles.

Regan forgets about the leak for the moment. He grabs the line. "Hey, I've got a bite!" *Food . . .*

16

There passed a weary time. Each throat
Was parched, and glazed each eye . . .
When looking westward, I beheld
A something in the sky,

Something's tugging at the
line — short sharp tugs. Regan gives it a quick jerk. The
line goes slack. "Lost it," he groans.

Another tug. "No, it's still there!" This time he waits
to let the fish take hold, then jerks the line again. He
yanks a small, silver blue fish clear out of the water. It
plops into the dinghy.

Flopping wildly about on the floorboards, it almost
flips over the side. "Don't let it get away!" Matt yells.
They both grab at it — miss. Regan finally catches it and
holds on tightly while he pries the pin out of its mouth.
The fish squirms in his hand. It feels slimy and its fin
pricks his thumb, drawing blood. "What do I do with it
now?" he asks.

Matt takes out his knife. "Give it here," he says, and
Regan hands over his prize, feeling sorry for the fish. He

turns away as Matt goes to work with the knife. He hears a cracking sound. "There, it's dead," Matt announces. Squishing sounds follow, and Regan keeps his eyes on the horizon.

"Who's first?" Matt holds up a strip of white flesh. "Regan? You caught it."

Regan hesitates but not for long. His stomach aches with emptiness. He takes the strip of flesh gingerly and tries to bite it. It's tough and chewy and fishy-smelling, but it does wet his mouth. He manages to swallow a morsel without gagging.

Carol reaches for a strip and tries it halfheartedly. She makes a face and puts it down. "Maybe if we leave it in the sun, it'll sort of . . . you know . . . cook a bit."

"Good idea," Matt says. He tosses the head and guts as far from the dinghy as he can, so they won't bring sharks. Then he lays the strips along the side of the dinghy, which is already heating up from the sun. "Maybe later I'll be ready to try some," he mutters.

The sun climbs higher. They sprawl on the bottom, hardly moving. Occasionally, one of them sits up and scans the horizon. Once Matt makes a sighting and they all leap up. It's a small patch of white in the distance — like the top of a sail. But it soon disappears below the horizon.

"Too far north," Matt mutters. "They're searching too far north." He gives up watching, goes to the stern and starts to fiddle with the outboard. He adjusts the needle valve and cranks the motor again and again. "No use. No life at all," he says in disgust.

Regan's trying to keep his eyes on the spot where the sail had been. *They must be out there,* he thinks, *maybe just out of sight.* He sits on the dinghy's rounded side, staring at the northern horizon, but the rubbery fabric is so hot that it burns his bare thighs. Eventually he gives up and stretches out on the bottom with the others, a jumble of sweating, sunburned limbs. He longs for evening to come and cool them off. At the same time he's afraid of what else evening might bring. *The shark? Another storm?*

Half asleep, a new sound penetrates his heat-dazed brain. A buzzing noise. He brushes his hand over his head to drive off the mosquito, or whatever it is. Suddenly he sits up with a start. *Mosquitos this far from land! Impossible!* He searches the sky, head swiveling.

There. A black dot to the north. *A plane!*

Matt and Carol hear it too. Regan points. "Over there, low on the horizon!"

Carol yelps, "Yes, I see it!"

"Me, too," from Matt. "Coast Guard plane, I bet!"

They wave jackets. They wave towels. The plane grows bigger. It seems to be heading straight for them. Closer and closer.

At the last minute, it banks and makes a 90 degree turn to the west. "No, over here! Over here!" they scream. How can it not see them? But the plane flies by, heading due west now, into the sun. Then they see it make another

90 degree turn and head back north. Soon it's just a speck in the sky again. Then even the speck is gone.

Regan looks at Carol. She turns away, eyes moist.

"Anyway, they've got a plane out looking for us," he says. "And it'll be back."

"Looked like it was flying a search pattern," Matt says. "Maybe tomorrow it'll come a little farther south."

They flop back down onto the floorboards in silence.

It will come back tomorrow, Regan keeps telling himself. *We just gotta keep afloat until tomorrow.* He sees Carol reach out and surreptitiously test the side of the dinghy. Her fingers sink in up to the knuckles

"You know those boring essays they make us write," he says suddenly. "Like in the fall when school starts again? 'How I Spent My Summer Vacation.' Just think of the great ones we'll be able to write this year!"

Carol considers for a moment. She giggles. "Yeah, I'll call mine, 'How I Went Snorkeling for a Day and Got Lost for a Week.'"

"Great title," Regan laughs. "What'll you call yours, Matt?"

"Not much good at essays."

"You can be this year."

"Yeah, maybe. Lots to tell, that's for sure," Matt admits, but he isn't really listening. He's staring intently at something in the water. "Watch out!" he warns, pointing. "Here it comes again."

Regan follows Matt's finger. A fin! Coming fast. *Right on schedule,* he thinks. *Late afternoon, just like yesterday.* But this time, he sees, the shark has company. Behind it are two more fins.

The lead shark comes on fast. When it reaches the dinghy, it doesn't waste time circling. It dives underneath, followed by the other two. The dinghy rocks as the sharks churn the water. They charge back and forth, mouths open. The water's streaked with blood and bits of torn flesh.

"It's the fish underneath!" Regan cries. "They're after the fish."

The dinghy bounces; the water boils with fleeing fish, streaking sharks, and blood. Then, quite suddenly, it's all over. The fish that aren't eaten are gone. The dinghy settles down and they wait tensely to see what the sharks will do next. A strong fishy odor hangs in the air.

Fish gone, the sharks circle quietly now, round and round, eyeing the dinghy. *Looking for more food,* Regan fears. *Now that they've tasted blood, they want more.* One bangs against the side.

Carol grabs the oar. "That does it!" She flails at the closest shark, scoring two quick hits on the nose. It backs off. The shark, Regan knows, could snap the oar in two with its powerful jaws if it wanted to. But it doesn't. It keeps its distance.

As the sun is going down, the sharks suddenly disappear. *Do they sense that the dinghy is slowly sinking?* Regan wonders. *Do they know all they have to do is bide their time?*

17

The silly buckets on the deck,
That had so long remained,
I dreamt that they were filled with dew;
And when I awoke, it rained.

The sharks have barely left when a new threat appears. Out of the dusk, Regan sees a line of low black clouds sweeping in from the east. The wind is rising, stirring up short choppy waves, which slap against the dinghy.

"A line squall," Matt warns. "It'll be fierce, but it won't last long."

The squall hits them like a runaway truck. It sends the dinghy spinning across the water, rocking crazily. The low clouds have rain in them, but the wind drives the rain so hard it comes at them horizontally. They have no chance to collect any. It's all they can do to hold on in the wildly spinning dinghy. Regan opens his mouth and manages to suck in a bit of the rainwater streaming down his face.

Then, as suddenly as it came, the squall passes. They

watch it go, chasing rain ahead of it and stirring the sea to the west. They catch their breath and slosh about in ankle-deep water. Matt scoops up a handful and tastes it. He spits it out. "Yuck! More seawater than rainwater." He begins bailing. "Hey, our fish strips blew away!"

There's no sign of them. Regan wishes he'd eaten more while he had the chance. But suddenly he notices that something even more important is missing. "The other oar's gone too!" he cries.

The dinghy looks empty without it. "Oh, no! Must've floated out during the squall," Carol moans. They stare wildly around at the sea. It's nowhere in sight. *Now what do we do when the sharks come?* Regan wonders. The most valuable thing they had left. Why didn't they tie it down? *Another mistake. How many are we allowed?*

Dejectedly, they go back to bailing. Then they settle down for another night at sea. *Our third night,* Regan thinks. *How many more nights can we survive?*

The squall had signaled a change in the weather. Regan wakes from a dream in which his gym teacher is making him stand under a cold shower. He jerks this way and that to try to get away from the icy stream, but it follows him relentlessly.

He surfaces to find it's raining steadily.

Carol is already awake, her mouth open, her face turned up to the sky. Matt, however, is still sound asleep, rain streaming through his tousled hair and running down his cheek. Regan shakes him. "Wake up, Matt. It's raining!"

He sits up, rubbing his eyes. "Wow! Rain!"

Stretching out the jacket between them, they lean back as the jacket fills and sags under the weight of water.

They take turns dunking their faces in the pool of rainwater and drinking. Regan can't get enough. Again and again he slurps the sweet water, soothing his parched throat. They all drink their fill. Matt belches loudly. "Ahhh," he sighs. "First belch in days. Sure feels good."

Satisfied finally, bellies stuffed with water, they collect more until the jacket's full again. Then they tip the contents into the jug, spilling most of it, giggling together in the rain. The downpour goes on and on, and they keep collecting until the jug is overflowing.

Eventually it stops raining and the clouds begin to clear. A sliver of moon plays hide-and-seek with them.

They're soaked through and shivering in the night air. Especially Regan. He bails vigorously, but even that doesn't stop his violent shivering. "Th-that's what I get for being s-so skinny," he says, laughing.

"It's no joke," Carol says, "You'll get hypothermia. Gotta warm you up. Come here." She makes Regan lie down. Then she lies beside him and hugs him to her. Embarrassed, he tries to pull away. "Don't be silly," she snaps. "I'm not enjoying this any more than you."

She makes Matt lie close-up against Regan on the other side, despite his objections. Sandwiched between them, Regan's shivering slows and finally stops, but he can't sleep. He listens to Carol's steady breathing. *She never seems to lie awake frightened and worried,* he thinks. But for him, this is the worst time: the middle of the night, the time when his mind goes round and round. *They'll never find us. They're searching too far north. The sharks will be back tomorrow. The dinghy's losing air. The next storm will sink us.* He can't seem to stop.

Not meaning to, he whimpers aloud, then tries to cover it up with a cough.

"You all right?" Matt's voice.

"I-I thought you were asleep."

"Can't sleep."

"You, too? Thought you could sleep anywhere."

"It's really scary out here at night."

Regan shifts so he can see Matt's face in the weak light of the moon. *He's scared too,* he thinks. *I figured I was the only one. I never thought Matt was scared of anything!*

"Think we'll ever get out of this?" Matt says.

He's asking me! Regan tries to think of something positive to say. All he can come up with is: "At least we've got water now, Matt. You can survive a long time if you've got water."

"I guess." Matt doesn't sound convinced.

They fall silent, listening to the waves slap against the side.

"Matt?"

"Yeah."

"About that time on the diving tower. Sorry I wimped out on you." It came out unexpectedly. He hadn't even known he was going to say it. But now it's out, he might as well keep going. "I really wanted to dive after you. I just couldn't." He takes a deep breath. "I get all trembly up on that tower. I never told anyone this before, but . . ." He hesitates, then plunges on. "You see, I'm afraid of heights. I can't even climb up a dinky ladder without getting scared." *There, I've said it.*

"That tower is awful high," Matt agrees.

"But you looked cool up there."

"I wasn't that cool. I just made myself do it. But I don't mind heights too much. I don't mind anything, as long as I'm . . . you know, in charge of what happens to me. But out here . . ." He pauses, struggling to express himself. "Out here, there's nothing I can do about it . . . nothing but hope someone will rescue us before it's too late. But how long's this dinghy going to stay afloat? I get spooked every time I think about that – and those sharks. Jeez, Regan, I'm really scared of them."

This is the most Regan's ever heard Matt say at one time. "I guess anybody'd be scared of them," he says.

"That's for sure," Matt says, "except maybe some hero in a movie. But this is no movie, this is for real."

The dinghy rolls sluggishly as a swell lifts it.

Regan can't let go of the subject he started. "I guess the guys are still laughing," he says. "I think about that day at the pool all the time."

Matt stretches, yawns. "Forget it, Regan. I have. Not worth worrying about. Doesn't matter anymore. We've got more important things to worry about now – a lot more important than what a bunch of guys back home think." He yawns again and closes his eyes.

Regan lays back and gazes up at the sky. The stars are beginning to show as the rain clouds scatter and the crescent moon sinks toward the horizon. One particularly bright star sparkles in the west. "Maybe the plane will come back tomorrow," he says.

There's no answer. He hears Matt's heavy breathing and looks over at him. He's sound asleep. *Matt doesn't stay scared for long,* he thinks. *He knows how to forget – lucky guy.*

He stares at the bright star in the west. It's yellow, golden yellow. *Wait a minute, that yellow color, isn't it? . . .* He finds the Big Dipper and traces the curve of the handle. Yes, that leads him right to the yellow star. *It is! It's Arcturus!* The brightest star in the summer sky. That's a good omen. Maybe a sign that they'll soon see the yacht named after the star.

His eyes go back to the Big Dipper. This time he follows the line of the two stars that make up the pouring end of the dipper. That leads him to the North Star, Polaris, low on the northern horizon. *Somewhere over there to the northeast, the searchers will soon be setting out again. Maybe tomorrow will be the day they find us.*

He yawns. Now he's sleepy too. As he closes his eyes, he thinks back to his talk with Matt and a new thought goes round and round in his head: *I'm not the only one who gets scared. Matt gets scared too. Maybe everybody's scared sometime, even Carol, even the toughest guys. It's not just me.*

18

What is the ocean doing?

From the deck of the blue cruiser, Anthony watches his grandfather motor slowly back. The old man's head is down, his shoulders sagging in the early morning light. Anthony's never seen him so low. He's tried to tell him it wasn't his fault, but no matter what he says, his grandfather still blames himself for letting *Arcturus* go off alone with a tropical storm approaching. "But you couldn't tell them what to do, Grandpa," he said. "And you were busy. You had those two boats to repair."

It didn't do any good. "Should have insisted they wait to see if the storm was going to hit before I let them go," his grandfather said.

Every morning his grandfather meets with the other skippers to talk about the search. Altogether there are five boats searching – *Arcturus*, the blue cruiser, two other boats belonging to friends of Anthony's grand-father, and the U.S. Coast Guard, which joined the search yesterday. By now they all know that the dinghy, if it's still afloat, would be more than a day's sail away. Only the Coast Guard vessel and the blue cruiser, with their powerful engines, can do daily searches that far out. *Arcturus* will continue to search but closer in, around the islands, just in case.

Now Nathan Waterman ties up his dinghy and climbs wearily back aboard the cruiser, shaking his head. "Those folks on *Arcturus* look worse every day," he says. "I doubt if any of them are getting more than an hour's sleep a night. It's a good thing they're kept busy all day."

"Anything different planned for today, Grandpa?" Anthony asks.

His grandfather shakes his head. "The Coast Guard thinks we're looking in the right area and it's just a matter of time. I don't know, though. I'm not convinced."

"Did you tell them what you were telling me last night?"

"I did, Anthony, but they don't seem ready to try it. Not yet anyway."

His grandfather is staring at a chart. The worry lines on his face have gotten deeper. "So why don't *we* try it, Grandpa? Just us two."

His grandfather looks up. "You know, Anthony, that's just what I was thinking." He jumps up. "Let's see. We'd need to take some extra diesel fuel. And I better radio the others and let them know what we're up to."

His movements are livelier all of a sudden. *He's his old self again,* Anthony notices, as his grandfather grabs the VHF and begins making calls, alerting the others to his plan.

They hustle to get everything ready to go. The sun is only just rising as they leave. Matt's father calls out from *Arcturus* as the cruiser passes. "Good luck, Nathan."

"And to you," Nathan Waterman calls back.

Once clear of the Cays, he gives the cruiser full throttle and it surges ahead, diesels throbbing. He swings the wheel until they're heading southwest.

Steering a southwest course means cutting diagonally across following swells, which is always tricky. Anthony watches, admiring how smoothly his grandfather handles the rolling seas. He has complete faith in him. *If anyone can find those guys, Grandpa will,* he tells himself. *He may get lost in Toronto, may seem like a befuddled old man in the city, but he knows the Caribbean like the back of his hand.*

But even if his grandfather is right about where the little dinghy might be, he knows they'll have to get awfully lucky to come across it in all that expanse of sea.

19

I woke, and we were sailing on
As in a gentle weather:

Regan wakes up at first light as usual. Right away he can tell the dinghy has lost more air. It sags in the middle where they are lying, and the stern, weighed down by the heavy motor, is only a few inches above the water.

The sea is quiet, the usual early morning calm. But he fears what will happen later when the wind and waves pick up. Already a breeze is sending cat's paws across the water toward them.

"Matt!" He shakes the inert body of his friend.

Matt opens his eyes, closes them again.

"You gotta wake up, Matt."

A groan. "It's hardly light yet."

Carol opens her eyes. "What's up, you guys?"

Regan shoves his fist into the side to show her. "We've lost more air. We've got to do something!"

She frowns. "What can we do?"

Matt's awake now. He sits up. "Yeah, you're right. Gotta get rid of some weight."

"Huh?" Regan stares at him. *What does he mean, "get rid of some weight"? One of us? Draw lots or something to see which one has to go overboard first?*

But that's not what Matt has in mind. "The outboard," he says. "Gotta dump the outboard."

Regan looks at the motor, gleaming in the morning light. "But it's worth thousands."

Matt shrugs. "It's no use to us. It's only weighing us down."

"We should try one more time to start it," Carol says. "Just in case."

She gets up, cranks the motor a few times. It's as dead as ever.

A wave slops in over the stern.

"That settles it," Matt says. He tries to unscrew the clamps holding the motor onto the stern board. They're on tight, the clamps frozen with salt. Another wave slops in.

Matt pulls out his sailor's knife, selects a stout spike from the assortment of blades and screwdrivers, and shoves it in the hole in the clamp handle to give him leverage. He grunts, going red in the face as he applies pressure. Suddenly the first clamp gives way and he almost tumbles overboard. He tackles the second clamp.

"Now we gotta lift this beast," he says. "Give me a hand."

Regan and Carol crowd around, trying to get a hold on the motor. But the weight of all three at one end is too much. The stern dips and water pours in.

"Quick, get to the bow, Regan!" Matt barks.

With Regan sitting on the bow as a counterweight, the stern stays just above the water. Matt and Carol stand one on each side of the heavy motor. They brace themselves. "One, two, three – heave!" Matt chants. They raise it a few inches. "Heave!" They gain a few more inches. One more "Heave!" and the motor is off. Now they have only to lift it clear of the stern and drop it overboard. But at that crucial moment, a wave rocks the dinghy.

They stagger; the motor falls onto the stern board with a crash. For a second Matt, Carol, and the motor are tangled in a heap, draped over the stern. Then the motor topples slowly over and disappears into the sea with a glug. Matt falls back into the dinghy, but Carol is half in the water, half in the dinghy.

"Carol!" Regan leaps to the stern, grabs her legs and pulls her in. She clutches her side, her face twisted, breathing hard.

"You all right?"

She winces, shifting gingerly to a more comfortable position. "It's my ribs. I fell against that board."

"Does it hurt a lot?"

"Damn wave! If it hadn't been for that . . . you okay, Matt?"

Matt is still sitting where he fell. He looks dazed. "Yeah. I guess." He massages his right shoulder. "Anyway, the motor's gone. Pass the water jug will you, Regan."

Matt takes the jug with his left arm. His right arm hangs uselessly at his side. He swigs from the jug then holds it out for Carol, but she can't raise her arms at all and Regan has to hold the jug for her. He tilts it until she signals she's had enough. He raises the jug to his own lips, but he's taken only one sip when he stops suddenly and blinks.

He's staring at the peak of a rocky island, jutting out of the sea a couple of miles ahead. For a moment he thinks he's seeing things, hallucinating from hunger. *A mirage.* He waits for the mirage to fade away, but it doesn't. It stays there, sticking out of the sea like the top of a mountain. *It must be real. We must have drifted toward it in the night.*

"Look!" he cries. "An island!"

Matt and Carol's heads snap up.

"Whoa!"

"Look at that!"

They forget the air leak, their hunger, Carol's cracked ribs, Matt's sore shoulder. They just stare, minds racing. Then, suddenly, they're all talking at once.

"Can you see any people?"

"Is that a house?"

"Will we drift to it?"

Regan squints over his shoulder at the sun, which has just cleared the horizon. "There's east," he says. "So the island's just about due west of us."

Matt, head swiveling, looks from the sun to the

island and back again several times. "A little north of west, I'd say. We could drift right to it. Or we could drift by to the south. Depends on the wind. And the current."

"Come on, current," Carol urges.

Seeing the island makes Regan long for the feel of land under his feet. He waits impatiently, staring hard, as if his stare could bring the island closer. The wind freshens, but the dinghy is so low in the water that the wind doesn't move it along like it did before. Time drags by.

By midmorning, the island is a lot closer. The sun is higher now and it's harder to tell which direction is which, but Regan begins to doubt they'll hit the island the way they're going.

By noon, it's obvious they won't. "We're not going to drift right to it, that's for sure," Matt says. "The current's taking us south of it."

"Oh, if only we get close enough," Carol says. A coughing spasm doubles her over in pain, clutching her ribs.

Close enough for what? Regan wonders. *She can't possibly swim with cracked ribs. Nor can Matt with one useless arm.*

He has only his hands to paddle with. He tries but the dinghy is so sluggish now that his frantic attempts barely move it. Carol can't help. Matt slips into the water and tries scissor kicking with his legs, pushing with his good arm. He soon gives that up. All they can do is wait – and hope.

Gradually the island looms larger. Thousands of birds circle the peak, noisily protesting their approach.

Seagulls, terns, and other birds with long white tails fly out, squawking, to look the intruders over.

Soon they can tell they're going to miss it by quite a bit. Drift right by to the south. At the base of the island, below a rocky cliff, they can see a thin strip of pebbly beach and a few scrubby trees. An old shack sags beside the trees. They shout. Regan pictures someone opening the door, stepping out, and waving. But no one does. The only answer to their shouts is the renewed shriek of the birds.

"Can't be anyone there," Matt says. "There's no boat."

Not even a dock, Regan realizes.

And as they get closer, they see that the shack is abandoned. Most of the roof is missing.

By the middle of the afternoon, they're abeam of the island, but well to the south of it. Regan stares despondently at the one piece of solid ground they've seen. So close yet so far. Finally he can't stand it any longer.

"I'm going to swim for it," he says.

20

Like one, that on a lonesome road
Doth walk in fear and dread. . . .
Because he knows, a frightful fiend
Doth close behind him tread.

Carol turns, startled. "Regan, don't be crazy!"

"I can swim that far. It's only half a mile or so."

"It's too dangerous."

He remembers the sharks and hesitates.

"And what good will it do?" Matt puts in. "There's no one there to help you."

"And you'd be alone there," Carol adds. "Marooned."

An image of Robinson Crusoe waiting years for a ship to pass by his lonely island pops into Regan's mind. *Maybe it is a crazy idea.* But when he looks up at that towering rocky pinnacle, he knows he has to get there somehow. *Someone* has to get there, and there's no way Matt or Carol can make the swim in their condition.

"We should stay together, so we can look after each other," Carol argues.

"But it's our only hope," Regan counters. "If I can get to the top, there's a chance the searchers will see me way up there. A lot better chance than down here."

Matt follows his gaze to the peak, with the birds wheeling around it – tiny white blobs. "You're going to climb way up there?"

Hadn't thought of the climb, Regan realizes. *Too busy worrying about swimming with sharks. But the way the sides of the dinghy are collapsing, there's no choice,* he tells himself firmly. He *has* to do it. Much as he hates to leave Carol and Matt. It's their only chance.

He steels himself: *first get to the island, then worry about the climb.* He stands poised, ready to dive.

Carol puts a hand on his arm to stop him.

"I can make it," he says. He wishes he was as confident as he sounds.

She sighs, resigned to him going. "Okay, but don't dive . . ." The rest of the sentence, "you might attract sharks," she leaves unsaid, but he knows what she means.

"Good luck," Matt puts in.

"You, too," Regan says. "See you soon."

And before he can change his mind, he slips into the sea and strokes strongly away from the dinghy.

He tastes salt, feels a jolt of adrenaline from the cool water. Counting to take his mind off sharks, he gets into his rhythm. Ten strokes, then a peek at the rock to make sure he's headed right, then ten more strokes, keeping his legs going. Suddenly he gets a shivery feeling that something is following him. His skinny legs feel vulnerable back there, as if something is getting ready to take a bite. He stops, unnerved, and looks back. *There's nothing there,* he scolds himself, *it's all in your imagination. The sharks don't come until sundown. Just keep going.* He starts up again

To keep his mind busy, he tries to figure out the distance he can swim in the pool at home. *Say the pool's a hundred feet long.* Stroke. *Twenty-five lengths, a hundred feet each length.* Stroke. *That would be twenty-five hundred feet.* Stroke. *That's nearly half a mile right there.* Stroke. *And I've done twenty-five lengths of the pool lots of times.* Stroke. *So I can easily swim half a mile.*

He sneaks another look. Still a long way to go. His arms feel like lead. *Maybe I figured wrong.* Stroke. *Why am I so tired?* Stroke. *Maybe it's a lot more than half a mile.* Stroke. *Maybe not eating for three days has something to do with it.*

He looks up again, sees that the current is carrying him off course, changes direction, and plods on. One arm, then the other, keeping his legs moving. A wave slaps him in the face and he half-chokes. He has to tread water till he can breathe again. *Think of the great marathon swimmers — Marilyn Bell, Florence Chadwick. They didn't stop just because they were tired.* He forces himself to go on. Stroke. *They didn't stop just because they got a mouthful.* Stroke. *Just because there might be something nasty, like eels.* Stroke. *Or sharks.*

Regan presses on. One arm, then the other, one arm, then the other. At last the island begins to grow larger.

A little larger each time he looks up. He swims with renewed vigor now. He's almost there.

With a last spurt of energy, he covers the final hundred yards. His toes touch bottom, then he's standing up, wading, ignoring the stones that dig into his feet. With a whoop, he staggers onto the beach and collapses on the sand.

21

The western wave was all aflame.
The day was well nigh done!
Almost upon the western wave
Rested the broad bright Sun;

He lies on the sand, panting,
dizzy, not sure he can even stand up. But he has to.
There's no time to lose. He drags himself to his feet, legs
shaking from fatigue. Shading his eyes, he looks for the
dinghy. At first he can't see it at all. Then a swell lifts it,
a tiny thing and two tiny figures, dwarfed by the sea
around them. *No wonder that plane didn't spot us.*

He waves at Matt and Carol, but the dinghy dips into
a trough and is lost from sight again. He isn't sure
whether they even saw him. How he wishes they were
here with him on this little bit of beach. They look so
small and helpless and far away. Less than a mile, but they
might as well be on the moon.

Already the dinghy has drifted past the island. *Soon it*
will be many miles away. And how much longer will it stay

afloat? He has to start climbing. He has to get to the top while there's still daylight. For their sake. Now.

He looks around. *Where to begin?*

There's nothing on the island except shrubs, crooked and weathered. And the old shack. He pushes on the door. It complains loudly and falls off with a crash. Inside are a few tattered scraps of fishing nets. Nothing else.

Staggering, his sea legs used to a pitching dinghy not solid unmoving ground, he picks his way along the stony beach. The rocky pinnacle seems to go straight up, but he finds one place where the face looks a little less steep. *As good as any,* he decides. He takes a deep breath, grabs one of the shrubs that sprout here and there from the rock, and begins pulling himself up.

As he climbs, the shrubs become sparser. He has to dig his fingers into crevices for handholds and grip ledges with his toes. He works himself higher, not daring to look down. Panting, he stops for a rest, then moves on.

A ledge crumbles underfoot. He freezes, pressing into the rock, feeling his heart flutter against his chest. A gull glides by, squawking at him, as if mocking his fear of heights.

He tilts his head back cautiously. Above him, a section of rock has been eroded so that it's less steep. He sees that climbing will be easier if he can get that far. Somehow he hauls himself up and, once there, he covers a lot of ground quickly. He feels better now.

As he nears the top, hundreds of gulls and terns circle around him, shrieking. But one last obstacle – an overhang just before the top — stops him cold. He crouches under it, looking up. How can he possibly scale that overhang?

A gust of wind tears at him. His nerve begins to slip away. He clings to the rock, trembling, sure he's going to fall, to be dashed on the beach below. He can't stop himself. He looks down.

Far below, long lines of surf roll in endlessly, like a TV screen that's out of whack. He sways dizzily and jerks his eyes away. *Concentrate on the top,* he tells himself. *Concentrate. There's got to be a way past the overhang.*

He works sideways, feeling for cracks with his toes. His trembling hands search blindly over his head for something to grip. They latch onto an unseen shrub. It's prickly but he clutches it in a death grip. *This is it — now or never.* He prays the shrub will hold his weight. Knees scrabbling against the overhang, he heaves himself upward with his last ounce of strength. The shrub holds and he rolls onto the top and lies gasping. His hands and knees are scraped and bleeding, but he doesn't care. He's done it.

The birds go berserk. They're all in the air now, screeching furiously. A gull sweeps by his head, barely missing him. He ignores it, picks himself up, interested in only one thing. He scans the horizon.

First to the north, where the search boats will come from. Nothing in that direction. To the east, nothing either. He chokes back his disappointment. He can see a long way from up here, but there's nothing to see. To the west, he spots the tiny speck of the dinghy. Beyond it, the sun is going down fast.

His heart sinks with the sun. He's reached the top too late – the searchers will be heading back to their bases now. They'll wait for morning light before resuming the search.

He knows he can't go through that climb again tomorrow. He'll have to spend the night up here. He shivers in the wind, missing his jacket. He was so anxious to get to the island, he didn't give a thought to what he might need. He has no water either. Not that he could have carried any on his swim.

It doesn't take him long to explore the top – a small area of ragged rock, not much bigger than their backyard at home. A few windblown shrubs are dotted about, and the odd loose boulder and some scraggly patches of grass. As he walks around his tiny domain, the birds became more frantic than ever, their calls even shriller. He hears a crack and feels something squishy between his toes.

He looks down at the broken shell of a speckled egg and cringes. He hates doing that to the birds. This is their home, not his. But he's so hungry that even that mess of raw egg looks good. Anything to put in an empty stomach. He can't resist picking up the broken shell, tilting back his head, and draining the gluey white and yellow stuff inside.

Once he starts looking, he sees clusters of eggs everywhere. He grabs another and cracks it on a rock.

Gulping it down, he reaches for another. A tern dives at his head, calling plaintively. He stops, looks at the egg hungrily, then gently puts it back where he found it. "Sorry," he tells the tern. "No more. I promise. Not tonight, anyway."

The sun has reached the horizon. He has to get ready for the night. Has to work fast while there's still light. Breaking branches from the shrubs, pulling up handfuls of grass, he arranges a bed of sorts behind a boulder where there's some shelter from the wind. He lies down on it and pulls some of the grass and small branches over him. The branches are scratchy and stick into him; the birds are still shrieking, but he falls into an exhausted sleep.

22

I moved and could not feel my limbs;
I was so light – almost
I thought that I had died in sleep,
And was a blesséd ghost.

When he wakes, he doesn't know where he is. It's dark, and quiet as a tomb. Then he remembers, and he starts to shake – from cold, from loneliness, from fear. He hears a sound. Was that what woke him? He sits up, listening, holding his breath. It fades away, then comes again. Like singing – a sad song, a lament. Ghostly. He's on top of a rock in the middle of the sea, alone. *Can't be anyone here. Must be the birds, or the wind. Mustn't it?*

Overhead, thousands of stars blink and glitter. He stares up at them. They seem so close, he feels as if he's climbed not just to the top of the rock but halfway to the stars. The Milky Way stands out clearly – a long narrow drift of stars. He remembers reading that there are a hundred *billion* stars in the Milky Way; our sun is just one of them. And the Milky Way itself is just one spiral arm of a galaxy, which, in turn, is just one of thousands of galaxies. Another galaxy, which he can see clearly now, is Andromeda, two million light-years away.

He imagines people on some planet in Andromeda looking at the earth right now through powerful telescopes. What they will see is the earth as it was before the last ice age. That's how long it takes the light to reach them. He likes thinking about things like that. The stars keep him company.

He hears the singing sound again and has a feeling something else is keeping him company too. It's a feeling he's never had before. Like there's another presence, even though he's alone on top of a rock in the middle of the sea. But it isn't scary, it's just there. Since the diving tower debacle, he's felt alone in the world. But not now. And yet here he is in the most remote place he's ever been. He doesn't understand it, but his shaking stops and he begins to feel calmer.

Scanning the sky he locates his old friend Arcturus – bright yellow – in the west. *What other stars are there this time of year? Something about a triangle. The summer triangle, that's it!* He lies back and studies the pattern of stars, trying to remember.

There! In the east. He gives a cry of triumph and traces out the triangle: Vega makes one corner, and . . . and . . . Deneb and . . . Altair. *That's it! The three stars of summer. One for each of us. Carol, Matt, and Regan.*

The birds are quiet now. They've settled for the night. He has to pee badly, but he doesn't want to stir them up again, so he tries to get back to sleep. No use; there's no denying the urge of his bladder. He pushes himself up stiffly and stumbles to a nearby patch of grass, which will at least muffle the sound. A few birds squawk nervously, but they stop as soon as he lies down.

The next time he wakes, the birds are definitely stirring, although it's still dark. He searches the sky, looking for Arcturus. Out here the stars guide him, like the compass helps him find his way on the boat. Arcturus is gone. It's below the western horizon, telling him the long night is almost over. Yet he knows sunrise will be a while coming.

He used to have the idea, if he thought about it at all, that the sun rose at dawn and that was that. But, in the dinghy, he has watched for the first time as night turned slowly into day. And he knows now that dawn doesn't come fast. Dawn takes its own sweet time. Especially when you're shivering and anxiously waiting, wondering if your sister and your cousin survived the night in the sinking dinghy.

The sky seems lighter already, but it's only the false dawn. *Like it's teasing you,* he thinks, because the sky then darkens again, even more so than before. What is it his teacher says? It's always darkest before the dawn. He knows what she means now.

Not until much later does the first faint hint of light appear on the horizon — as if someone has turned on a lamp in some far-off room. Impatiently he watches the pale light spread slowly upwards. Still no sign of the sun. He hugs himself for warmth and waits.

Gradually the fringe of light turns pink, the pink deepens to orange, and then, at last, the sun peeks over the horizon. Shyly, at first, as if making sure the coast is clear, then bolder until, suddenly, it seems to shoot up like a cork from under water. Clear of the horizon now, the sun is on its way for the day. It's time.

He stands up and stretches his aching joints. Then he picks his way to the edge of the rock and finds a perch facing northeast to begin his vigil. It will be from that direction the searchers will come. If they come. If they aren't still searching too far north. Occasionally he turns and glances west. There's no sign of the dinghy. He knows it's too far away to see now, even from this height.

The sun is in his face, warming him at last. He sits with his back propped against a boulder, staring out to sea, fighting the drowsiness that comes over him in waves, like it sometimes does at school in social studies. But this time Mrs. Gettel isn't there to scold him when he falls asleep.

He wakes with a start – as if his subconscious knows he has to wake up, knows there's something out there. And the first thing he sees when he opens his eyes is a flash of light, far away, to the northeast.

He shades his eyes and scans the sea, where he saw the flash. There it is again! Just a quick flash. *Some sort of signal light?* he wonders. And now he can make out something else — a moving dot on the water. Suddenly he realizes what the bright flashes are: the sun reflecting off a windshield as a boat dips and rises with the swells. *A searcher at last?*

Will they see him? *Oh, hurry, hurry,* he breathes, *before it's too late for Carol and Matt.* He stands, hopping from one foot to the other in excitement as he waits for the boat to draw closer. Suddenly he can't wait any longer. He races along the cliff edge, waving for all he's worth, though the boat is still many miles away. Maybe they'll see him anyway, he thinks, silhouetted against the sky.

Something bright would help. Something bright to wave. He looks down at his red swim trunks, hesitates, then bends and strips them off.

Naked, he jumps up and down, screaming and waving the red trunks. The commotion makes the birds wilder than ever. "Come on, birds, shriek!" he shouts. They shriek. Circle and shriek. Circle and shriek. Round and round they go. Up and down Regan leaps.

Suddenly he sees the distant speck make a sharp turn and head towards him. "It's coming!" he shouts to the birds. "It's coming!" Just to be sure, he keeps on waving until his arms feel as a though they'll drop off.

Gradually the speck grows larger, becomes a cruiser. A blue cruiser. With two figures in the cockpit. One of the figures lifts an arm and waves back, then Regan knows for sure they've seen him. This is it, what he longed for, what he was beginning to doubt would ever happen. They have found him.

Whooping for joy, he pulls on his trunks. But he knows he has one more trial to face. The climb down.

At the edge, looking down, the vertigo comes back with sudden force. He sways, pulls back. How he wishes he was at the bottom already. He tells himself there's nothing for it but to begin. He checks once more that the cruiser is really coming, and trembling, he kneels down and lowers himself over the edge.

The worst is getting past the overhang at the top. Gripping the same shrub he used to haul himself up, he lowers himself cautiously, feeling for a toehold below. He finds one, gets both feet on it, then comes the moment he has to let go of the shrub. Grabbing an outcropping of rock with one hand, he inches down, hugging the cold rock, feeling his cheek scrape against it, not daring to look, hardly daring to breathe.

Then, suddenly, he's past the overhang and he can breathe again. After that it gets easier. Now every move takes him lower instead of higher. When he reaches the steep section near the bottom, he tackles it eagerly. A sense of exhilaration fills him as he makes the last little jump onto the beach. He's done it.

The blue cruiser sits offshore, engine idling. Regan watches Anthony climb into the dinghy and motor the hundred yards to shore. He cuts the outboard, tilts it, and glides up on the beach. Regan runs to meet him.

Halfway there, his legs buckle and he collapses.

"Regan!" Anthony races to him. Regan looks up at his friend. He sees the concern on his face.

"Sure am glad to see you, man," Anthony says. He takes Regan's arm and helps him to his feet.

"Not as glad as I am to see you," Regan says, trying to walk.

"Easy, man, easy," Anthony urges. "Just lean on me."

They walk slowly to the dinghy. Anthony keeps looking back with a puzzled expression. "But where's your sister? And Matt?"

"Still in the dinghy. Tell you later. We got to find them fast."

There's something else he wants to tell Anthony right now. "Remember that day walking home from the pool, when you told me about the Caribbean?"

"Yeah, I remember."

"About the trade winds, and your great-uncle who disappeared, and your grandfather bashing sharks on the nose?"

"Yeah."

"Saved our lives. Sure glad you knew all that."

Anthony grins. "You probably know more about the Caribbean now than I *ever* will."

Regan grins back. "I doubt that. It took you and your grandfather to find us. Nobody else could."

Then Anthony shoves the dinghy off the beach and they climb in.

23

For the sky and the sea, and the sea and the sky
Lay like a load on my weary eye,

Anthony's grandfather leans over the side, wraps his strong arms around Regan, and hauls him aboard.

"Thank God we found *you* anyway!" he says. "Are you all right, Regan?"

Regan nods. "I'm okay, Mr. Waterman, but —"

"You look dehydrated and half starved, poor boy," Mr. Waterman interrupts. "We'd better get you some food and some water before we do anything else."

But there was only one thing on Regan's mind. "Carol and Matt, . . ." he begins.

"You don't have to talk about them now if you don't want to." Mr. Waterman's face is solemn. "Must have been awful for you, losing your sister and your cousin."

"But they're still in the dinghy!" Regan bursts out. "We've got to find them. It's sinking!"

Mr. Waterman blinks. "But how did you get? . . ." He stops. "Never mind. You can tell me later. Which way do we head?" He slams the cruiser into gear without waiting for an answer.

Regan points. "The dinghy was drifting southwest, near as I could tell. It passed the island yesterday afternoon. I was the only one who could get ashore."

"Good lad. We'll find 'em." Mr. Waterman guns the engine and wheels the cruiser around the island. He set a southwest course at top speed. "You go below with Anthony, Regan. You need food and rest."

But Regan pictures the dinghy with the sides collapsing, and he thinks of the terrible night Carol and Matt must have had. *If only it stays afloat a little longer, just a little longer.* "No, I'll stay up here till we find them," he says stubbornly.

Anthony stops halfway down the companionway and looks back. Then he shrugs and keeps going. When he reappears, he's balancing a tray with a box of soda crackers, a jar of strawberry jam, a tall glass of orange juice and another one of water. "Just a start," he says. "I brought you a shirt and hat too. Looks like you've had enough sun for a while."

"Enough for the whole year, I think," Regan says, reaching for the glass of water. He downs it in one gulp, then spreads jam on a cracker with shaking hands.

"Take the wheel a minute, Anthony," Mr. Waterman says. "I'll use the shortwave radio to let them know we found Regan. Keep a sharp lookout, boys."

Regan stares so hard at the sea ahead his eyes blur. With every wave he wills the dinghy to appear; with every wave he's disappointed.

Mr. Waterman returns and takes over the wheel. He swings it expertly and the cruiser glides up and over a big swell. "Your folks have been frantic with worry, Regan. They've been out in *Arcturus* from dawn to dusk every day. A bunch of other boats are searching too, and the Coast Guard. They've got a plane looking for you."

Regan hangs on with one hand as the cruiser rolls, stuffing crackers in his mouth with the other. "We saw the plane, but it never saw us," he tries to say, but he ends up with a coughing fit, spraying crackers. *Slow down, you don't have to eat them all at once,* he tells himself. He takes a drink of juice. "The plane turned back north just before it got to us."

Mr. Waterman nods. "Everyone's been searching too far north. The Caribbean current does run northwest mostly, so that's the way they figured you'd drift." He checks the compass and corrects his course. "Usually they'd be right, but there are side currents down here near South America and I figured there was a good chance the storm took you into a side current. And once you get in one, a side current can keep taking you south."

"So that's why they couldn't find us!"

"The search didn't seem to be getting anywhere, so Anthony and I decided to slip down here and have a look. But we still wouldn't have spotted you if you hadn't climbed that rock." Mr. Waterman smiles. "When we saw those birds all stirred up, we knew something was up."

"I kept telling the birds to make a racket," Regan says. "And they sure did."

"But how did you get to the island anyway?" Anthony asks. He has his eyes glued to the sea ahead.

"I swam." Regan tells about Carol and Matt hurting themselves when they tried to dump the outboard, and how the dinghy drifted right by the island. And once he gets started, it all pours out — about the rogue wave the first night and the sharks and the dinghy leaking and his desperate swim and his climb. The only thing he doesn't mention is his fear of heights. He hopes he's overcome that — at least made a start.

They listen without interrupting. "Well, Regan," Anthony's grandfather says, when he's talked out, "not many could have done all that. You should feel proud of yourself."

Maybe I will, Regan thinks. *But only if we find Carol and Matt.*

"It's lucky you drifted close to the Island of Wandering Souls," Mr. Waterman says. "It's one of the few islands around."

Regan starts. "It's called the Island of Wandering Souls?"

Mr. Waterman nods.

"Why is it called that?"

Mr. Waterman steps up onto the cockpit bench, steering with his right foot while he peers anxiously to

port. "Thought I saw something over there. Guess not."
He steps down again. "Why is it called the Island of
Wandering Souls? Well, a long time ago, before my time,
a family lived there. They made their living fishing, but
one day the father went out in his boat and a storm came
up. He never returned. The family waited and waited.
Every day the son climbed the rock and sat watching for
him. Months went by. Some other fishermen offered to
take them to the mainland, but they wouldn't leave. They
grew old there and one by one they died. It's said their
souls are still there, waiting for their father to come back."

He's quiet for a moment, then continues. "A
fisherman friend of mine stays overnight there sometimes. Says he's heard sounds in the night – like singing,
sad songs. Others say it's just the wind."

Sad singing, that's what I thought it was too, Regan
muses. *Didn't sound like the wind to me.* He's thoughtful as
he continues to watch the sea ahead.

Mr. Waterman glances at his watch. "Should be catch-
ing up to the dinghy soon. I figure they'll be right
around here somewhere." He throttles back to cruising
speed. "I'll radio for the search plane if we don't find
them soon." His brow is knit with worry lines. "I'll
never forgive myself if anything's happened to them. I
should have made you wait in Bequia until that storm
was past."

"It was my fault, Mr. Waterman, not yours," Regan
says. "Soon as I saw the storm cloud that day I should

have called the others back. Instead, I went snorkeling."

"Don't be hard on yourself. Any boy would have done the same thing."

But what's my father going to say? Regan wonders. He sits staring at the sea, wishing his father was as understanding as Mr. Waterman. *Anthony's lucky to have him for a grandfather.* He tries to remember his own grandfather, who died when Regan was small. But all he can come up with is a dim recollection of a stern, unsmiling man.

A flock of storm petrels appears out of nowhere and skims across the bow. At the same moment, from somewhere in his memory, an image of his grandfather floats up. They're at the dinner table, his face is close to Regan's, his eyes are flashing, he's scolding him for something . . . what was it? He can't remember. For not eating his vegetables maybe. But one thing he knows for sure, the anger in that voice scared him half to death. That's all he can remember of his grandfather, but it suddenly seems important.

A shout from Anthony interrupts his thoughts. He leaps up, hopes soaring. Anthony is pointing excitedly. "There! On the starboard quarter!"

"Where?" Mr. Waterman calls. "Where? I don't see anything." Regan can't see anything either. Nothing but waves.

"It's them!" Anthony insists. "Slow down."

For a moment Regan thinks Anthony must have been seeing things. Then another swell lifts the dinghy out of a trough and there they are, in front of him. The pitching dinghy is riding so low in the water, it's barely afloat. He sees Carol trying to stand, hugging her ribs; Matt waving frantically with his good arm.

Relief floods through Regan.

As Mr. Waterman maneuvers the cruiser closer, Carol beams at them, her sunburnt face half hidden by strands of salt-caked, bedraggled hair. Beside her Matt stands stolidly, like a rock, despite the heaving motion of the dinghy.

Getting them aboard isn't easy. Again and again, the waterlogged dinghy is slammed against the cruiser by the swells, then snatched away. It has to be timed just right. Regan stands beside Anthony, ready to reach for them.

"We'll grab you first!" Anthony shouts to Carol. "Next wave."

The dinghy lifts. At the peak of its upward thrust, they each grab an arm and haul her bodily onto the deck. She screams, "My ribs!" But she never stops grinning. She falls against Regan and hugs him. He squeezes her affectionately and finds his eyes filling with tears.

They haul Matt into the boat the same way. He flops onto the deck like a landed fish. Picking himself up, he grabs Regan's arm, then Anthony's. "Wow, you guys came just in time!"

Mr. Waterman fusses over them, tries to shoo them below to rest, but they're too excited to leave the cockpit.

They both crowd around Regan. "When you waved at us from the beach," Carol says, "I thought it was the last time I'd see you."

"Yeah, me too," Matt adds. "Did you *really* climb to the top of that rock?"

So Regan has to tell about his climb and his night on the rock all over again. "But it wouldn't have done any good," he finishes, "if Anthony and his grandfather hadn't decided to search down this way. They're the ones who saved us."

Mr. Waterman sees that both Carol and Matt have used up all the adrenaline that was keeping them going. They're suddenly so weak, they can hardly stand upright. He insists they go below. "Anthony will look after you," he says firmly, "while I head for home."

This time they don't argue. But, as they meekly file down the companionway, Regan stops. "What about the dinghy, Mr. Waterman?"

"Forget the dinghy. Let's get you home."

Regan looks at Carol and Matt. They look back at him. They all begin protesting at once.

"Please, Mr. Waterman. Please bring the dinghy."

"We *can't* abandon it now."

"Can't we tow it, please Mr. Waterman?"

But he shakes his head. "It's too deflated to tow. It would slow us down too much. The important thing is to get you kids back." He reaches for the throttle. Then he sees the stricken looks on the three faces and hesitates.

"I can haul it on board easy, Grandpa," Anthony says quickly.

His grandfather sighs. "Well, I suppose so. Quick, then."

Anthony rigs up a rope and pulley and soon has the dinghy lying on the deck. It sags like a deflated balloon, but its name still shows defiantly between the folds – *Discovery*.

"*Now* can we head for home?" Mr. Waterman says, reaching once again for the throttle.

24

A sadder and a wiser man,
He rose the morrow morn.

The growl of the engine and the thump of the bow on a wave are the first sounds Regan hears as he surfaces from a deep sleep. He looks up at the ship's clock above his head. *Four, already!* He's been sleeping since ten this morning.

He glances across the cabin. Matt's sprawled on a mattress on the floor, his mouth open, breathing heavily. Carol's sleeping peacefully on the settee, hugging a pillow. They all fell asleep right after breakfast – a breakfast he'll never forget. Nothing that different, but it seemed like the greatest food he'd ever eaten in his life. Scrambled eggs and ham cooked up by Anthony, and toast and marmalade. He could have eaten three or four platefuls. His stomach kept calling out for more, but Mr. Waterman said they had to take it easy. Not too much at once.

He rolls out of the bunk, moves to the companion-way, and pokes his head up. Anthony sets down a line he's splicing and grins at him. "Hey, it's the man."

"Almost there, Regan," Mr. Waterman says from behind the wheel.

Regan is surprised. Just since breakfast, all that distance that took them four days and nights in the dinghy. He climbs awkwardly up the steps to the cockpit. He feels the aches and pains now – the blisters from sitting in seawater, the stiffness, the sunburn, the cuts on his hands and feet from the climb.

"I called on the radio with the good news," Mr. Waterman says. "Going to be quite a crowd to meet you."

Regan blinks. "A crowd?"

"Yeah, man," Anthony says. "You guys are famous."

"You're kidding."

"It's been on the news every day," Anthony tells him. "'Three Teens Swept out to Sea in Dinghy.' 'Search Goes On.' Stuff like that. Isn't that right, Grandpa?"

"That's right," Mr. Waterman agrees. "You're big news. There'll be so many reporters there, we'll be lucky if we don't get run over in the rush."

Regan still wonders if they're kidding him. "But what did we do?"

Mr. Waterman says quietly, "You managed to survive in a small dinghy for all that time, with nothing but a few towels and a jug of water."

Regan absorbs this silently.

The outline of an island looms in the distance. "There's St. Vincent up ahead," Mr. Waterman says. "Better wake up Carol and Matt, Anthony. They won't want to miss this."

Anthony disappears below and when he comes back, Carol and Matt are following him, rubbing their eyes and yawning. As they stagger up the companionway, Regan wonders if he looks as much of a wreck as they do. Matt has come out in blisters and his arm is in a sling. Carol's salt-caked hair sticks out in all directions and dead skin is peeling from her face and arms and legs. She moves carefully to the cockpit bench, nursing her sore ribs.

Just as she's about to sit down, the boat rocks and she misses her aim and sits on Regan. He grimaces. "*You* sure didn't lose much weight, Carol!"

"But *you* sure did," she shoots back, grinning. "Your legs are so skinny, it's like sitting on two sticks. You gotta eat more, Regan."

Matt remains standing, gently rubbing his blistered backside. "At least you guys can sit down," he says. Regan and Carol laugh. Matt joins in. And once they start, they can't stop.

Anthony watches, bemused, then he begins to laugh too, and soon they're all laughing uncontrollably, even Mr. Waterman.

A small plane comes out to meet them. It circles and Regan sees someone taking pictures out the window. As they near the harbor, a fleet of boats streams toward them.

"What's going on?" Carol asks. "Carnival or something?"

Mr. Waterman tells her what he told Regan.

"They want to see *us*?" Carol asks, openmouthed.

"You're headline news," Anthony says. "Better get ready for a heroes' welcome."

"Heroes!" Matt exclaims. "We were dummies!"

Mr. Waterman smiles. "No use fighting it, kids. Better just give in and accept it. Everyone's trying to tell you how glad they are you made it back."

The boats are all around them now, the photographers calling to them to pose together. Mr. Waterman has to throttle back as they enter the harbor among the crowd of boats – every kind of craft that floats – yachts, trawlers, dinghies, kayaks, even an old raft with some kids on it. Many of them have photographers aboard, flashing pictures.

The photographers must have commandeered every boat in the Grenadines, Regan thinks. He scans the fleet. *No sign of them yet.*

Then he hears a familiar voice. "Over here!" It's his mother. *Arcturus* is anchored off to one side of the harbor, away from the crowd. She's waving one minute, dabbing her eyes with a tissue the next. Uncle Ron and Aunt Shelley are beside her, waving excitedly. *But where's my father?* Regan wonders.

The cruiser pulls alongside *Arcturus,* and eager hands help Carol, Matt, and Regan aboard. They're hugged over and over again. Anthony and his grandfather come aboard and they're hugged too. Soon they're all talking at once. Regan punches Anthony on the arm. "Maybe now you can show me around St. Vincent."

But someone is still missing. "Where's Dad?" Regan asks.

"He couldn't stop crying," his mother says. "He was so embarrassed, he went below." She's crying too, but laughing at the same time. "Go and get him, Regan."

He climbs down the familiar steps of the companionway. His father is standing in the head, drying his face with a towel.

"Dad?"

His father turns. He doesn't say anything, just takes a step to the doorway and, for the first time Regan can remember, he folds him in his arms. Then he steps back and looks at his son. "We thought we'd lost you...." His voice breaks and he smiles crookedly.

Through the hatch, Regan hears the photographers calling him out for more pictures. His father shifts his feet. "Must have been terrible out there, son."

Regan thinks for a moment. "Kind of, Dad." He wonders how to say it. "But I learned a lot too."

His father clears his throat. "I hope so. You know you should have come back before that storm hit." He can hear the same old edge creeping into his father's voice.

"That isn't what I meant," Regan says quietly. He sees his father look up in surprise. *I meant I learned about myself,* he wants to say. *I learned what I can do when I have to. And I learned a lot about my sister too.* He wants to say all that, but he doesn't know how.

"Dad!" Carol appears and her father embraces her. She puts her arms around the two of them. "Did Regan tell you how he rescued us, Dad?"

"Regan rescued you?"

"Sure," Carol says. "He —"

Regan interrupts. "But it was Carol who saved us from the sharks."

Their mother calls down to them. "You'll have to tell me all about it later," his father says. "We'd better go up now."

Regan stays where he is. "One thing, Dad."

His father stops, looks back quizzically.

"I'd like to bring the dinghy back to Toronto. Will you lend me the money to ship it? I'll cut lawns or deliver papers or something to pay you back, I promise. It's just that I'd like to have the dinghy around, and I know Carol would too. It'll remind us of . . . you know . . . a lot of things that are important."

His father frowns. "Ship the dinghy? That big thing? All that way?"

"It's not that big when it's deflated," Carol points out. "We can pack it in a box."

"Don't know why you'd want the thing around anyway," his father grumbles. He turns and clumps up the companionway steps behind Carol.

For a minute Regan continues to stare after him. *Still the same,* he thinks. *He hasn't changed. Doesn't bother me so much anymore though. He did cry and he did hug me.*

He closes the door of the head, turns on the tap full blast and fills the sink to the brim. *Water, fresh water, just by turning on a tap! Miraculous.* He supposes he'll soon take it for granted again. That and three meals a day and snacks in between and a comfortable bed with sheets.

No, the memory of those days may fade, he thinks, *but it will always be there. Especially with the dinghy in the backyard to remind me.* He splashes cool water on his face and neck and glances in the mirror. He considers the face looking back at him – the cracked lips, burnt nose, gaunt cheeks.

"And you're not so gutless after all," he says.

The End